BACK IN THE SADDLE

Blazing Eagle Ranch I

PEYTON BANKS

Your past was never a mistake if you learned from it.

— UNKNOWN

❧ I ❧

"**A**re we there yet?"

"Tyler King, you just asked me that two minutes ago," Maddy responded firmly. She had to put a little more emphasis on her words to let her nine-year-old son know she meant business.

"I know, but you said 'not yet,' so I didn't know when we'd be here," Tyler replied.

Smartass.

She guided her car down the road to her mother's home.

Finally.

The house she'd grown up in came into view. She turned into the driveway and parked behind her mother's vehicle.

"We are officially here." She glanced into the rearview mirror and stuck her tongue out at him.

He giggled and reached for his bag.

Her son was the apple of her eye. Just the sight of him had her smiling. She could never stay mad at him for long. With his infectious grin, steel-gray eyes, and his faithful Stetson on his head, her heart melted instantly.

She couldn't separate Tyler from that hat. It had seen better days. He was infatuated with cowboys, and on a whim two years ago, she'd purchased the hat. Not a day went by that it wasn't perched on his head. When he'd first gotten it, it was big, but he'd grown into it.

Maddy focused her attention on the house and sighed. She couldn't believe she had moved back to Shady Springs, Colorado.

Two weeks ago, she and her young boy had packed up their apartment in Colorado Springs and relocated to her hometown.

It had been one of the hardest decisions she had ever made in her life. She had tried to make a decent life for them in the city. A single mother could only do what she could, and the decision to move back to Shady Springs was what was best for them.

With the rising costs of living in the city not being met by her salary, the choice was solid.

Maddy had feared Tyler wouldn't do well with the move. He was leaving all his friends at school and their old neighborhood behind. She tried to prepare him as best as she could. Visiting her mother was different than permanently living there.

But Tyler had surprised her.

The minute he'd heard they were moving to the country and he would be near cowboys, he'd practically dragged her to Shady Springs.

"Let's go, buddy. Nana is waiting for you." Maddy exited the vehicle and blew out a deep breath.

Tyler stepped from the car with his duffle bag in hand. It was his slumber bag to stay over at his grandmother's while she went to work.

"Took y'all long enough," Myla called out from the porch.

Tyler sped off, running up the stairs to hug her. The relationship between Maddy and Myla was a strained one, but Myla believed in family and offered to help Maddy in any way she could.

"Someone couldn't find his favorite pajama pants and wouldn't leave until he found them." Maddy chuckled. When her son grew attached to something, it was a code red situation if he lost it. She walked around the car and up the stairs.

"That's all right. I have plenty for Tyler and me to do while you're at work," Myla said. She opened her arms to Maddy.

Maddy wrapped her arms around her mother in a tight embrace. The two of them had been through so much. Since her father died, it had been just the two of them.

Things had been tense in their family when her father was alive. He'd been the town drunk, and they never knew which version of Robert King they'd encounter when he came home. Maddy remembered the night they'd gotten the call that he had been found facedown in a puddle of his own vomit in an alley near his favorite bar he frequented.

Maddy was almost ashamed to admit she had been relieved. She loved him, but as his drinking increased, he wasn't the same man who rocked her to sleep to ward off her nightmares as a child.

He'd changed, and it hadn't been for the better.

"Go inside, little boy." Myla pulled away from Maddy. "Dinner is almost ready. Go put your bag away in your room and wash up. I even baked some cookies for dessert."

Maddy smiled at the excitement on Tyler's face.

"Have a good day at work, Momma," he said. He slammed into her for a quick hug.

Maddy cherished these moments. She removed his hat to allow her to place a kiss on his forehead. He glanced up at her with those gray eyes of his. It pained her every day to look into them.

They were the exact same color as *his,* and were a daily reminder of the one who had broken her heart.

Tyler tore away and ran into the house.

Maddy laughed and shook her head. She had to admit, Myla was a better grandmother than she'd been as a mother.

Maddy was okay with that. She couldn't change the past.

Tyler was her future, and that was all that mattered.

She was just grateful their relationship was on the mend. Her mother agreeing to watch Tyler helped keep babysitting costs down. Maddy had taken a job at the local bar as a bartender. Ironic, she knew, since her father was a drunk, but the wages were more than fair, and the tips were decent.

Working the late shift guaranteed she made extra. Here in Shady Springs, there wasn't much for locals to do but go drink and dance. Any more than that, they would have to head toward the city.

"You've done such a wonderful job at raising that little boy, Maddy. I'm proud of you." Myla leaned against the pillar behind her.

"Thanks," Maddy murmured. She wasn't sure where this was coming from, but she was willing to take it. Being a single mother was hard, and she played it by ear. Every decision she'd ever made, she tried to keep Tyler's best interests in mind. "That means a lot, Mom."

"I know I wasn't the best parent." Myla sighed. She folded her arms in front of her. "I truly tried my best with what I was dealt."

"I know." Maddy tucked her dark hair behind her

ear and turned to face the street. Her gaze swept the area. Not much had changed since she'd moved away all those years ago. Shady Springs was a small town, and most people stayed put. Those who left rarely came back.

Myla quietly stared at her. Maddy instantly grew uncomfortable. She knew what her mother was about to say before she even opened her mouth. This was a conversation she dreaded to have with Myla.

"When are you going to tell him?" Myla asked quietly.

"Tell him what?" Maddy feigned ignorance.

"You know what I mean, Maddison King. When are you going to tell that boy he's a daddy?"

Maddy rolled her eyes. "He's not a boy. He's a grown man."

"A man who deserves to know he fathered a child," Myla snapped.

"He didn't want anything to do with me then, so why does he deserve Tyler?" Her vision blurred from the tears teetering on her eyelids. She blinked, and they burned a warm trail along her skin. She wiped her face with the back of her arm, angry she could be brought to tears so quickly from something that had happened almost ten years ago.

"Maddy, I didn't mean to make you cry." Her mother moved to her side. Myla rested a hand on Maddy's arm. "We have to think of what is best for Tyler."

"I'm what's best for Tyler," she retorted.

Her mother's lips pressed together in a firm line, as if she wanted to say something else.

"Okay." Myla held up her hands. "I don't want to fight. I've made my feelings known, and it is up to you to do what you feel is best for your son."

Maddy glanced down at her watch. "I have to go."

Maddy jogged down the stairs without saying another word. She climbed into her car and put the key in the ignition. She cranked the engine, and when it roared to life, she put it in reverse and pulled out of the driveway.

Without looking back, she sped away, holding back tears.

It had taken her years to get over Parker Brooks.

She'd thought leaving Shady Springs would have helped, but it hadn't. His career as a bull rider had put him everywhere. Every time she'd turned the television on, he was there. He had flourished, and was one of the top bull riders around, becoming a household name.

He had it all—money, fame, and women.

He'd lived the high life while she'd struggled to provide for her son.

She was over him.

"Hey, Derek," Maddy called out, entering The Tipsy Cow.

"Hello, Maddy," he replied from his perch near the door. The after-work rush would soon be arriving. Derek, one of the bouncers, ensured everyone had a good time. He helped make sure the girls in the bar were watched when the crowd got a little too rowdy.

She kept going, beelining toward the locker room. She entered and arrived at her locker.

"Hey, Maddy."

She turned to find her friend, Debbie, standing at hers. Deb was a beautiful redhead, with the brightest blue eyes Maddy had ever seen. The woman was shy, and it was a wonder she could work in a bar where she had to interact with massive crowds.

"Hey, Deb. Sorry, I didn't see you standing there." Maddy placed her purse on the shelf.

"Everything all right? You looked like you had something on your mind." Deb shut her locker and walked over to stand next to Maddy.

Their friendship dated back to high school. They hadn't remained as close when Maddy had up and relocated to Colorado Springs. They spoke once in a while, just for old time's sake. Once Maddy had decided to come back, she'd reached out to Deb, who'd instantly offered to help her get a job. A word from Deb, and Maddy was hired.

"Oh, you know, everything. Like if this move back

home was the best thing for Tyler and me." Maddy shrugged. She grabbed her black apron and tied it around her waist.

"I'm sure it is. At least for now."

Maddy paused and smiled. Deb was right. At least for now, she could work, save money, and concentrate on her online classes. Maddy had help with Tyler, and that was a relief. She would just have to take it a day at a time. So far, Tyler was loving it here. Anytime they passed a ranch or a cowboy on a horse, he went wild.

"I don't know what I would have done without you," Maddy admitted. She shut the door and leaned against the row of lockers.

"Who, me?" Deb snorted. "Please. Any of the bars here would have hired you. With your experience in a big town doing this job, they would have been stupid *not* to hire you."

"Well, let's make sure they get their money's worth out of me tonight." Maddy laughed. Moving back from a larger city to a small town did have its perks. She was familiar with some of the popular drinks the college kids liked to order. That made her a commodity amongst the younger crowd.

"You're going to have to teach me some of those tricks, you know," Deb said. They left the locker room. "I may need to try my hand at bartending instead of waitressing."

"Stick with me, my friend." Maddy dramatically

waved her hand in the air. "As my apprentice, you shall learn it all."

They fell into a fit of giggles as they made their way out into the bar.

Tonight, Maddy was going to have fun. She wasn't going to think about her little spat with her mother, and she wasn't going to think about her son's father.

Maddy was going to have a good time at work while making some excellent tips.

$\maltese$ 2 $\maltese$

Country music blared through the speakers. Parker sat in the passenger seat of his brother's truck. Weary, he ran a hand along his face. He was tired. His damn knee was killing him, and they wanted to take him out for a few drinks.

Just shoot me now.

Carson and Wade were forcing him to hang with them against his will. He was sure there was some law out there that would protect him if he shot his younger siblings.

It wasn't that he didn't love them, because he did. The three Brooks brothers were as close as could be.

Tonight, Carson and Wade insisted they go out to their favorite hole-in-the-wall for a celebration of sorts.

It was all a bunch of horseshit.

Parker didn't think celebrating pregnant cows was

worth it, but Carson and Wade wouldn't hear any of it. They were just looking for any excuse to hit the town.

"Can you stop moping, please?" Wade asked. "You look like we are about to put you out to pasture."

"After the day we had, we deserve a few drinks," Carson spoke up from the back seat.

"All I want is sleep," Parker muttered.

"And you will. It will be assisted by a nice whiskey." Wade snorted.

Parker released a sigh and settled back in the plush leather seat. Any other day, he would be relaxed and joking around with them, but today just wasn't that day.

"Plus, the two of us couldn't go out alone. People would be wondering where the third Brooks was. We have a reputation to uphold," Carson said.

"And I don't feel like having to explain where Parker is." Wade snickered.

Parker shook his head at his siblings and bit back a smile. They were wearing him down.

The Brooks brothers were known throughout the county. It wasn't just the fact that they came from one of the wealthiest ranching families in the state, but they had earned a reputation from their drinking and fighting.

"Well, fine. A few drinks. We need to be on our best behavior tonight." He deepened his voice. As the eldest

Brooks, it was his responsibility to take care of his brothers.

"Oh, don't give me that shit, Parker." Wade grunted. "If I recall, half the fights we've gotten into was because of you."

"Hot-headed Parker." Carson chuckled. "But I have to say, there's nothing like a Brooks ass-kicking."

Parker tipped his hat to that. Between him, Wade, and Carson, the town knew they didn't take any shit. Not in business dealings, and certainly not in any other aspect of their lives.

"It has been a while," Wade murmured. He slowed the truck and turned into the lot of The Tipsy Cow.

"Hell, no. Not tonight. Just a few drinks, maybe some food, and that's it." Parker shifted in his seat to look at them.

"Fine." Carson sighed dramatically in the back. "We'll do it your way, Gramps."

Wade parked the vehicle, and they exited the truck. The three of them were built similarly. Each stood six-foot-three-inches tall and had broad shoulders. Their mom and pops had them working the ranch by the time they could walk.

Parker and his brothers had been early developers while growing up. They'd always been taller and stronger than their classmates. According to Pops, it was just good genes.

"I'll buy the first round of drinks, boys," Wade

announced. He clapped Parker and Carson on their shoulders.

The line to get into The Tipsy Cow was lengthy. Thankfully, the Brooks boys never had to wait to get in anywhere.

"Hey, Derek, how's it going tonight?" Parker stalked up to the door.

"Going swell. Y'all go ahead in." Derek gave a nod to Parker. "What's up, Wade? What's up, Carson?"

His brothers greeted Derek before they all stepped inside the bar. Parker bit back a curse at the crowd. The music was loud, and the drinks must already be flowing. There was a small throng of people on the dance floor.

They headed for the table they always sat at whenever they came to hang out. They were regulars here, and anyone who had a brain knew that.

Parker's gaze locked on two young boys with barely enough fuzz to call mustaches sitting at their table.

Parker stopped in front of it. Wade and Carson stood next to him. The three of them glared at the two idiots.

"This is our table," Parker growled. His damn knee was bothering him something fierce tonight. If he was forced to be here, then he was going to sit at his damn table.

The guys scrambled away, vacating the seats. Parker walked to his chair in front of the wall. Wade and Carson each took their seats. Carson turned his baseball cap around and leaned back in his chair. Wade ran a hand through his thick brown hair before grabbing the drink menu.

Parker pulled his Stetson down farther on his head. It was his favorite hat, and he'd be damned if he took it off. There were only a handful of times when it came off.

When he entered his momma's house.

Showers.

Sleep.

Any other time, his hat remained on his head.

"Now I hope you fellas are here to just have a good time." Jerry, the manager, stopped by the table. He had a serious expression that told them he meant business.

"We're just looking for some good food, drinks, and music tonight, Jerry." Carson smiled.

"Yeah, you said that last time—"

"And we paid for the damages," Parker cut him off. He was irritated, and didn't want to hear shit from the manager.

"Like we always have," Wade chimed in.

Jerry eyed them. "No trouble tonight, fellas," he warned. He spun on his heels and walked away.

"Hey, boys. How are you?" Their server, Sonya, appeared. She'd worked at The Tipsy Cow for years. "What can I get you tonight?" she asked, but she had eyes only for Wade. She was practically eye-fucking him, but Wade wasn't paying her any attention. His gaze was on the dancers.

She was a pretty girl, but she did nothing for Parker.

"Whiskey. The bottle," Parker replied. "And whatever my brothers want."

Wade and Carson placed their orders, adding in some appetizers.

"I'll be back shortly." She cast one last, longing look in Wade's direction before she turned and walked away.

The Brooks brothers were used to the attention of females. They were handsome, muscular, and wealthy.

Parker was no different. On the circuit, he was never alone if he didn't want to be. There were plenty of bunnies who tried to bed a successful bull rider. He'd been through so many women over the years, but there was only one who had caught his heart and broke it in two.

Parker blinked. There was no use in going down memory lane. That ship had sailed a long time ago.

Wade and Carson were rooted in a conversation on the number of pregnant heifers they had counted. Bets were being tossed back and forth on how many live births they would end up with.

"Here you go, fellas," Sonya announced. She set Parker's whiskey bottle down in front of him, along with a glass. She handed Wade and Carson their drinks before stepping back. "Food should be up soon. Anything else you guys need?"

She did this thing with her eyelashes that made Parker think something was in her eyes.

Or was she trying to catch Wade's?

Parker shook his head and reached for the container. He poured himself a healthy amount of the amber liquid into his glass.

A popular country song came over the speakers. Screams echoed through the air as some women ran to the dance floor.

Maybe his brothers were right. They needed to get away from the ranch to relax and celebrate. The number of heifers pregnant was a record for them.

Parker glanced over at the people dancing. Quite a few women were out there, extremely tipsy, trying to dance sensually, causing him and his brothers to laugh at the ones who ended up on the floor.

Parker finished off his drink and poured himself another one. By this time, Sonya had dropped off their appetizers.

He was enjoying the time he was having with Wade and Carson. The Tipsy Cow had the best bar food around. He even found himself chuckling with his brothers.

"I'm serious. Dr. Hutson could not get his arm out of the damn cow," Carson cackled.

Wade tipped his chair back, chuckling at their younger brother.

"What do you mean he couldn't get his arm out?" Wade asked.

"Doc checked her and confirmed she was pregnant. Then he goes to pull out, and his arm was stuck up to his damn shoulder." Carson, at this point, had tears running down his face.

Parker barked out a hefty laugh.

Dr. Guy Hutson had been the local vet in the area for the past five years. He'd taken over his father's practice when the elder Dr. Hutson fell and broke his hip. After his recovery, the elder doctor decided to work out of the office and allow his son to handle all the farm animals.

"So, what did he do? Just stay there?" Parker asked. He dragged his fries through the ketchup on his plate, then ate them.

"He said something about her being swollen inside, and he had to just maneuver his way out of her." Carson shrugged.

Life on a ranch was never dull.

Parker finished the last of his wings and reached for a napkin. He wiped his hands and snagged his empty glass.

A sharp whistle cut through the air. He glanced up to find Carson staring off at the bar.

"Well, I'll be damned. Look who is working at the bar," he said.

Parker followed Carson's gaze and froze in place.

Maddison...fucking...King.

His hand tightened around his empty glass. He grabbed the whiskey container and poured himself a double.

"When did she move back?" Wade asked, his eyebrows rising high.

Parker was also curious. He sensed his brothers gazes on him, but he refused to look at them. He stared down at his glass and the amber liquid inside of it.

As much as he didn't want to stare at her, he couldn't help it.

He peeked back in her direction.

Her lips were curved up into her beautiful smile. The years had indeed been kind to Maddy. She was thicker than he remembered. Her top was black and off the shoulders. He couldn't see any more of her, but what he could see, he liked.

Fuck.

His cock thickened. He ran a hand along his jawline, unable to believe that just by seeing Maddy, he still responded to her. Almost ten years had passed, and he reacted like a young man wet behind the ears.

He gripped his glass and knocked back the liquid.

His gaze traveled back to her again. He couldn't see

who she was talking to, but all he knew was that he wanted to plow his fist into the guy's face.

"You gonna go over and say hello to her?" Wade asked.

Parker cut his gaze to his brother. "Nope."

He poured himself another drink.

Why the hell did she come back? She'd been in such a rush to leave before, so what made her reappear in Shady Springs?

"I thought you said two drinks?" Carson asked, tipping his chin to the bottle in front of Parker.

"We're here to celebrate, right? Then let's fucking celebrate." Parker's words dripped with sarcasm as he raised his glass in the air. He readjusted his hat, but he couldn't tear his gaze away from the bar.

He was feeling the effects of the alcohol. He wasn't driving, so he didn't have to worry about that. He knew, without a doubt, his brothers would make sure he got home safe and sound.

Maddy appeared comfortable doing her job. She joked around with the other barmaid while mixing drinks. Maddy was the star behind the bar and was drawing a crowd. She moved around the small area as if she'd been doing it for years.

"Not going to say anything to her, yet you're staring at her." Carson chuckled.

"Fuck off," Parker growled.

He sat back and looked out at the dancers, but he

was no longer interested in watching them. The television held no interest. Drag racing was on. Usually, he'd be glued to the TV, but tonight something—no, someone—caught his attention. He glanced back at the bar, and some asswipe was getting handsy with Maddy.

Parker pushed back his chair and stood.

"What the hell?" Carson's head swung around toward the bar. "Aw, hell."

"Well, shit. I guess Parker's going to say hi after all." Wade stood.

Parker didn't feel any pain in his knee, thanks to the alcohol. He readjusted his Stetson and stalked toward the bar.

"How about tomorrow night, Maddy?"

Maddy tried to keep her smile friendly. Billy Houston sat at the bar with a buddy she didn't recognize. She and Billy had gone to high school together. He'd been the football jock who was supposed to go somewhere.

From what Maddy had heard, he'd made it to college and lost his scholarship for a reason no one talked about.

He was back home working his father's ranch.

"Billy, I just moved back into town. I'm working a lot, and just don't have time to date right now." She tried to let him off gently, but this was the fourth time he'd asked her out in the last hour. She was starting to get a little irritated.

"That's hogwash, and you know it," Billy snapped. He snagged her wrist, and this time wasn't letting go.

"I'm sure there are a ton of women out there who would love to go out with you." She pointed out onto the dance floor.

Derek stood by the door with his watchful eye on her. One word, and Derek would come plowing through the bar to get to her. They had grown up in the same area, and had been friends when they were kids. He'd graduated a year before her. He worked at The Tipsy Cow part-time, along with holding a job as a deputy at the sheriff's department. He was the size of a linebacker, and she was surprised he'd never played football after high school.

"Fine. If you won't go out with me, how about you fix me another drink?" He released her.

"Sure. Same thing?" Maddy asked. Her wrist throbbed slightly. She held back, rubbing it, and prayed she wouldn't bruise from Billy's grip.

He grinned. "You know how I like it, darlin'."

She spun on her heel and grabbed the top-shelf scotch. She poured him a double and made a mental note to cut him off after this. It was jam-packed for a Friday evening. Maddy wasn't going to complain since the tips were going to be out of this world tonight. Everyone was having fun, and when that happened, the tips added up quick.

"Here you go, Billy," Maddy announced. She set his drink down on the counter in front of him.

He reached into his wallet and slapped a crisp twenty-dollar bill onto the bar.

Maddy's gaze flickered to the bill before meeting Billy's. "I'll go get your change." She snagged the bill at the same time Billy snaked his hand out and gripped her wrist again.

This time painfully.

"You think you are too good for the likes of me?" Billy snapped. He tightened his hold on her.

"Billy, you're hurting me," she gasped.

"Why did you leave? 'Cause Parker boy didn't want you anymore?" He laughed.

Maddy froze in place. The color drained from her face.

"If you want to leave with that hand, you better let her go," a familiar voice growled.

Maddy glanced at the newcomer, and the bottom of her stomach dropped.

She couldn't breathe.

She recognized the low drawl, that worn-down hat, and the firm set of the jawline. It had been years since she'd seen Parker, and it took her right back to the last time she'd seen him when she was nineteen years old.

He was older now, appeared harder. There were more lines on his face. He was still tall, but now filled out his button-down cotton shirt quite nicely.

Two other imposing figures appeared behind Billy.

Carson and Wade.

Their faces were just as dark with fury as their brother's.

Tod, the other bartender, cursed beside her.

Billy let her go and swiveled around on the stool to face Parker. He stood, but was still shorter by about four inches. Parker's face was murderous, and Billy must have had too much alcohol to realize he was staring down at a bull about to charge.

Maddy swallowed hard.

The Brooks brothers were not the ones to pick a fight with.

"What the fuck do you want, Parker boy?" Billy drawled.

"I think it's time that you leave, Billy," Parker warned him. His voice was low and menacing.

The sound of it gave Maddy goose bumps.

"Who the hell are you to tell me to leave? I'm just having a little fun here, just like everyone else," Billy taunted. He turned to his friend. "Ain't that right, Joe?"

"We sure are," Joe quipped. He apparently wasn't from around Shady Springs if he didn't know who he was dealing with.

"This is the last time I'm going to warn you," Parker said. He rested his elbow on the counter. The look was casual, but the vibes radiating from Parker were anything but.

"What? Why do you care if I talk to Maddy? I'm just making a play for your leftovers," Billy continued.

Maddy fell back against the counter, unable to believe what was coming out of Billy's mouth.

"Shut up, Billy," Tod snapped. He grabbed Maddy and pulled her away from the men.

"What did you say?" Parker asked, moving closer. Nothing could fit between them. "I didn't quite catch what you said."

"I mean, if you had her, she has to be good, with all the women you've been blowing through." Billy laughed.

Parker may be a big man, but he indeed moved like lightning. Billy didn't see the punch coming.

All hell broke loose.

Maddy was yanked to the back room, away from the melee by Tod. Screams filled the air, along with the sound of glass shattering. Tod glanced out through the window of the swinging door and snickered.

"It's been a while since the Brooks brothers tore up the bar together." Tod chuckled.

"What?" she asked, flabbergasted.

Parker and his brothers were still tearing up bars together at their age?

"Not as often as they used to." Tod peeked through the window and winced. Something crashed beyond the door on the floor.

Billy should have kept his mouth shut.

Maddy leaned back against the wall and ran a hand through her hair. This was unbelievable. She had the situation handled just fine. She was just about to signal to Derek when Parker showed up.

Where the hell had he come from?

She hadn't even known he and his brothers were in the building. The bar was at full capacity, and it was hard for her to see past the people crowding the bar. She had been so engrossed in doing her tricks and mixing her drinks with the flair she'd picked up in the city.

Maddy let out a deep sigh. Why would Parker come to her defense? In all the years she'd been gone, not once had he tried to contact her. Her eyes pressed closed as memories surfaced.

She bit her lip tight, remembering that day. She had gone over to The Blazing Eagle Ranch to see Parker off. He was going down to Texas and would be gone for a couple of weeks.

———

Maddy knocked on the door. Her nerves were shot. She had some news she needed to share with Parker. It couldn't wait until he got back home. She wanted to tell him now before he left so they could celebrate when he returned.

Jonah Brooks opened the door. "Yeah? What do you want?"

Maddy automatically took a step back. Her heart raced at

his hard glare. She knew Jonah didn't care for her. Heck, she didn't think he liked anyone who didn't have the last name of Brooks.

"Hello, Mr. Brooks. Parker asked me to meet him here today before he left," she said, finally able to find her voice. She offered him a smile, but all he did was grunt back at her.

He stepped out of the house and slammed the door shut behind him. He appeared larger than life. He was a tall, stocky man, with weathered skin and steel-gray eyes that all of his sons had inherited.

Maddy gulped.

She hadn't really spent much time with the elder Brooks before, and today was not the day she wanted to. Parker had always steered her away from his father as much as possible.

Jonah Brooks was the meanest son of a bitch in the county. She watched him move over to the edge of the porch and fold his arms across his chest.

"So, my boy wanted you to come to see him off, did he?" Jonas glanced over at her for a second, then turned back to the land before him. He leaned against the pillar on the porch and let out a deep breath.

She nodded. "Yes, sir."

"You and Parker have been hanging pretty tight. You like him?"

"Yes, sir, I do. Parker is the sweetest guy I know." She clasped her hands in front of her. She wasn't going to divulge any other feelings that she had for Parker.

Did she like him?

She was in love with him.

He'd swept her off her feet the moment they'd first met. They had been inseparable for the last six months they had been seeing each other. Parker took her out on the range, trying to teach her to ride a horse. She was deathly afraid of the beasts.

He'd paired her with a sweet mare who loved sugar cubes and apples. Parker had told her it would take a while before the fear would be gone, and then she'd be completely comfortable.

She didn't know if he was telling her the truth, seeing how he loved to live dangerously. She didn't know how he could hop on the back of a bucking bull.

She'd gone to a few of his practices, and she just about had a coronary watching him in the ring with the huge bulls. Their horns alone could impale a man and take his life.

And, of course, Parker loved it.

He was really good at it.

"Is that so?" Jonah asked. He turned and faced her. "How's that daddy of yours?"

She blew out a shaky breath. She hated it when someone asked about her father. They all knew how he was. Robert King was an alcoholic, the laughingstock of the town. She had begged her mother to leave him. They could do better without him.

But Myla had refused.

She didn't have any skills to get a job, for she had been a housewife and stay-at-home mother.

Arguments were constant in the home. Maddy hated being there. The air was always tense, and for a young woman of nineteen, it had her thinking of moving out soon. She was technically grown. She could get a job and start out on her own.

Spending time with Parker gave her that escape from a bad situation. The constant bickering was wearing down her sanity.

With Parker, she could forget all of that. He was her breath of fresh air. He'd quickly become her constant.

"My father is...my father, sir." She didn't know what else to say. What was she going to do, lie? Jonah would see the truth.

Everyone did.

Robert King drank himself into debt. His checks went to booze. There were plenty of times their family went without electricity. Momma had to go to the food bank to ensure she and Maddy had meals on the table.

"Hmm..." Jonah murmured. "Sorry to hear that, girl."

"You don't have to be. It's not your fault," Maddy replied bitterly.

The wind blew gently, pushing her hair into her face. She tucked the offending strands behind her ears.

"Well, I didn't want to be the bearer of bad news, but Parker's not here." Jonah turned to face her.

"What?" she sputtered. "What do you mean he's not here? As in, he's coming back before he leaves?"

She looked at the door to the house. That couldn't be correct. Parker promised she'd get to see him off.

"There had been a change in plans, and Parker had to take an earlier flight, but I would have thought he'd have told you himself."

"Umm...okay. When will Parker be back? The same day as before?" she asked. She'd just have to speak with him when he returned.

Jonah pushed a hand through his hair, which was the same color as Parker's. "Listen here. You seem to be a nice girl. Parker didn't know how to tell you that with him going on the circuits, there isn't going to be time for romancing and dating. He needs to focus on his career."

Maddy froze in place.

No time for romancing and dating?

She blinked back tears. She had thought what they'd had between them was special. They hadn't said the love word to each other yet, but Maddy was pretty confident it was coming.

Or, at least, she thought it had been.

She'd been so wrong about Parker.

"So, what are you saying? He's dumping me through you?" Her voice ended on a squeak. Her gaze blurred from unshed tears.

"I sure as hell didn't want to do this. My son didn't know how to tell you that whatever y'all had going was a passing fancy. Cut your losses now, girl. The relationship wouldn't have worked." Jonah shook his head and glanced back at the horses grazing off in the distance. "Men like Parker draw more women than honey does flies. You wouldn't be able to handle what comes with life on the circuit. If you are as smart as Parker claims, go. Leave. Walk away and don't think twice about my son. He needs to concentrate on his career, anyway. He can't afford to be brought down to your level."

Her level?

Wow, that was like taking a knife to the heart.

Unable to speak, she just nodded and walked down the stairs. She could barely see her way to her mom's car.

Maddy got in and blew out a deep breath. She wouldn't cry in front of Jonah. She started the car and turned it around, heading down the driveway.

She thought she'd found the pot of gold at the end of the rainbow.

Instead, she'd found cold, darkness, and pain.

She gripped the steering wheel tight. She left The Blazing Eagle Ranch, heartbroken, four months pregnant, and alone.

❧ 4 ☙

"I ought to have the three of you thrown in jail," Derek bellowed. He arrived in front of Parker and his brothers. The muscular deputy eyed the three of them. "You were warned about causing trouble tonight. We've had enough of y'all coming in here and destroying property."

"We know. Just calm down," Wade interjected. He moved in front of Parker with his hands raised.

At the moment, Parker was glad his brothers were there. Wade could be the more reasonable person.

"Jerry is going to have to close down to have the place remodeled after what you boys did in there." Derek pointed to The Tipsy Cow.

Parker leaned back against Wade's truck. He took his Stetson off and shoved his hands through his thick hair. The anger was still boiling inside him.

"Well, next time you and your men need to make sure drunks aren't harassing the staff," Parker drawled. He put his hat back on. He swayed slightly, still feeling the effects of the whiskey and adrenaline.

"I had my eye on Billy. Maddy said she was fine," Derek snapped, angling toward Parker. "The bartenders and I have a system. I don't need you doing my job."

Parker pushed off and stood eye to eye with the bouncer. "You sure? Him hurting her wasn't handling it. You weren't fast enough, Derek. The crowd was too thick. He could have broken her wrist before you got to her. Is that how we do things around here? Let someone get hurt, then react?"

"Cool your jets, Parker, before you find yourself spending the night in a cell," Derek warned. His eyes narrowed on Parker while his nostrils flared. "I can still have the three of you arrested. Hell, you reek of alcohol. It might do you some good to spend the night in one."

Parker dove for Derek with a growl, but two strong arms snatched him back.

"Let's go, big guy." Carson stepped between Parker and Derek.

"Let him go, Carson. Hit me if you want, Parker. I'll lock your ass up for assaulting an off-duty police officer," Derek threatened.

Wade stepped in front of Derek. "We got him, Derek."

Carson pushed Parker back to the other side of the truck. "No one is going to jail tonight."

"Here, I'll write a check right now to Jerry. We know we did wrong, and we're willing to fix this," Wade offered. He motioned for Derek to walk with him. "Just take me to Jerry, and I'll make this right."

The two of them marched away, but not before Derek shot Parker a hard glare. Parker wasn't one to back down, and held it until they disappeared into the crowd.

Parker glanced down at his busted knuckles. They were swollen, and turning black and blue. He winced when he tried to squeeze his hand shut into a fist. Nothing seemed to be fractured. As for Billy, Parker was pretty confident he'd shattered the idiot's nose.

He'd seen red when he saw Billy touching Maddy.

Billy, you're hurting me.

Maddy's words still echoed in his head. He should have damaged more than Billy's nose. Just the thought of her getting hurt at the hands of a punk like him was enough to break the beast inside him loose.

The feeling of Billy's nose crunching under his fist was temporarily satisfying.

The deputies from the sheriff's department had arrived to break up the fight. The men had rushed inside and pulled Parker off Billy. The cops had the bar cleared out in minutes. They were currently ordering the crowd that lingered around the parking lot to leave.

"Is it broken?" Carson asked.

Parker shook his head. "No, but it hurts like hell."

"It's worth it." Carson chuckled. He held up his hand, and they had matching busted knuckles. "That Joe guy just did not do it for me. People around these parts have no respect."

Parker grunted. He searched the parking lot for any sign of Maddy or the bartender who'd dragged her away from the brawl.

He needed to speak with her. He thought he'd gotten her out of his mind, but one look tonight, and Parker was thrust back in time when all he could do was think about her.

They had unfinished business.

"I got to go back in there," he muttered. He pushed off the truck, intent on going back inside The Tipsy Cow. He had to find Maddy. If he had to pull her out of there himself, he would. She owed him an explanation for her sudden disappearance.

"Oh, hell no. They are not going to let either of us in there." Carson blocked him and pushed him against the truck. "Just sit tight here until Wade comes back, and then we'll head to the ranch."

"I just need to speak with Maddy," he snapped. He narrowed his gaze on his younger brother. He may be older and have a limp, but he was sure he could still whip his brother's ass.

"Don't look at me like that. I am not the enemy." Carson folded his arms in front of him.

He glanced around his brother to see if she'd come out of the bar. She'd ran from Shady Springs, and he never knew why. He didn't want to believe what his father had shared with him, but then she'd left. Cut every level of communication they had.

He'd come back from Texas, high on his wins. Imagine his surprise when the one person he wanted to celebrate with was long gone.

Packed up and disappeared.

Now she was back.

Smiling and carrying on in the bar as if nothing had ever happened.

And, dammit, sexy as ever.

But she hadn't wanted him. Parker bit back a growl. She hadn't even had the decency to tell him herself. To look him in the eye before she'd left.

No, she'd waited until he had hit the road and left him.

Parker was unable to believe his father. When he'd arrived at her home, and her mother confirmed she'd moved and wouldn't give him her new phone number, it had finally hit home.

So, he did what he knew best.

Rode bulls.

He'd sunk himself into his career, riding the toughest

bulls he could find. It had been dangerous, but he didn't care. It brought him more money. The feel of the mighty beast underneath him was like an aphrodisiac.

He couldn't get enough of the adrenaline rush.

Those precious seconds to hold on and show the beast who was in charge.

It became everything to him.

He lost part of himself then with drinking and lots of women, but his career flourished. He became a legend. He'd thought he was invincible, until his injury.

A busted-up knee that, after quite a few surgeries, left him with a limp and unable to ride anymore. He'd returned home with his tail between his legs.

But his father hadn't let him sulk for long. He was a Brooks, and they had a ranch to run. It was his father's legacy to pass it down to his three boys, and he needed all of them to be committed.

So, Parker did what came naturally to him. He got on his horse and threw himself into The Blazing Eagle Ranch.

Carson tapped him on the shoulder. "There goes Wade."

"I need to speak to Maddy. Just give me five minutes." He took a step toward the bar.

"Derek is not going to let you in. Hell, we almost got banned, period. I had to put a little extra money on the damn check." Wade stalked back to them with a scowl. He pointed to the car. "Let's go home, boys."

Carson slapped Parker on the back. "Come, big bro. Let's get you in the truck."

Parker returned Wade's scowl. He didn't know when his younger brothers had become so bossy.

Parker allowed Carson to guide him to the passenger door. Before he got in, he glanced one last time at the bar to try to catch a glimpse of Maddy.

Parker settled back in the seat. Carson shut the door behind him and hopped in the back. The engine roared to life. The truck swayed as Wade pulled it out of the parking lot, maneuvering the vehicle onto the street.

"Brooks brothers at it again." Carson chuckled.

Parker no longer felt playful. He shoved his hat down over his eyes, not wanting to laugh and joke with his brothers any longer.

"Music?" Wade asked.

"No," Parker growled. He shifted in his seat with a grunt. He privately willed the ride to go by fast.

He was just in a sour mood, and there was nothing that would dig him out of it.

The cab remained quiet for the ride home. Wade and Carson always knew when to back down and leave him be. He'd stew in his anger, and by morning, he'd be back to his usual self.

The vehicle rocked, and Parker recognized the dip in the road. Wade had turned down the way that led to their homestead. Within minutes, the truck drew to a halt.

"You gonna be all right getting into your house?" Wade asked.

Parker pushed his hat from his eyes and saw they were in front of his house. On The Blazing Eagle, their family had enough land where each son was able to build his own home. One day, the ranch would be left to the three of them, and as long as a Brooks was alive, a Brooks would live on the property.

Jonah granted them each their own corner of the land. Parker's home was east, Wade's south, and Carson's was on the west side. The main house where their father lived was located on the northern part.

"Yeah, I'm good." Parker coughed. He opened the door and climbed out. He winced, and had to pause for a second.

His knee was stiff as a board.

"You sure?" Carson asked, getting out of the truck. He walked up to the passenger door.

"I said I'm fine," Parker snapped.

Damn alcohol had worn off. Parker continued on and let out a curse. His limp was more pronounced. He didn't know if it was the actual injury, or maybe he was just getting old, and a bum knee didn't make it any better.

He reached into his pocket and took his keys out. He stumbled up the stairs and was able to insert the key into the lock. He turned and waved at his brothers, who were still parked, watching him.

Wade hit the horn and drove off down the gravel drive.

Closing the door behind him, he kicked off his boots. That was one thing his mother, Grace, God rest her soul, had engrained into him.

"When you enter the house, Stetson and boots are left at the door," Grace would say. "No telling what shit you've dragged in."

Parker headed for the kitchen. He opened the freezer and lifted out a bag of frozen vegetables.

The coldness stung for a second on his busted knuckles. He made his way to the family room. He left the lights off, not needing them.

He'd built this house from the ground up, and knew it like the back of his hand.

His feet carried him to the bar. He grabbed the container of whiskey and poured himself a hefty glass.

"I'm getting too old for this shit," he muttered. He took a seat in his favorite recliner, located in front of the large bay window. He positioned the frozen vegetables on his hand again and hissed.

He brought his glass up to his lips and took a sip while memories of Maddy floated to his mind.

She'd been so beautiful and free-spirited. She'd given Parker her innocence. Seeing her back, he vowed to find out why she had returned to Shady Springs.

"**S**top running!" Maddy called out after Tyler, who promptly ignored her. She chuckled, observing her son running over to the aisle where the cookies and snacks were. She was off today, and she looked forward to spending it with Tyler. They would run some errands first before returning home. She promised to take him to the park, and then he promised to play her favorite board game with her tonight.

It was mother-son day, and they always made the best of it. Maddy cherished these moments. She just prayed that once Tyler grew up, they would remain close and have special time put aside for the two of them.

Glancing down at her list, she aimlessly pushed the cart. She was on a budget, as always. Being back in

Shady Springs gave her a little wiggle room, but she still had to be very mindful of what she purchased.

"Mom, can I go pick out a cereal?" Tyler asked as he walked over to her.

She glanced down at the basket and saw they had collected everything on the list.

She bit her lip.

Could she let him pick out a box of cereal instead of buying the one she knew was on sale?

Tyler stood by the cart, patiently waiting for her.

Her heart melted. It was hard to tell Tyler no.

Her boy was such a good kid. She'd splurge today for him.

"Sure, sweetie."

"Thanks, Mom!" he shouted and ran off.

"No running!" she hollered out once again. She'd made the right choice. Something so little as picking out any cereal he wanted was a big deal to a nine-year-old.

Cereal meant they would need milk.

Crap! She spun the cart around and headed toward the refrigerated aisle.

"How the hell did I forget to put that on the list?" she muttered to herself. They could never keep milk in the house. Tyler drank it like his life depended on it. It was no wonder why he was so much taller than the average nine-year-old. Milk was obviously good for the bones.

She turned the corner and came to an abrupt halt at a familiar figure standing in front of the milk. That height, the dark-brown curly hair, those wide shoulders. Maddy's heart raced. It couldn't be. Not today. He looked around as if feeling someone staring at him.

She blinked. Her body relaxed slightly.

Wrong Brooks brother. It was Wade, not Parker. It was scary how much the brothers resembled each other.

Swallowing hard, she made her way to him.

"Mornin'," Wade drawled.

Maddy drew up the courage not to run away. She paused her cart near him and offered a small smile. "Morning, Wade. How are you?"

"Not bad. You doing okay?"

"Yeah, I'm fine." She shook her hand in the air. "I hate to say that I'm used to things like last night happening. I guess you can say it comes with the business. But I do want to say thank you for stepping in."

"No need to thank me. Billy and Parker were going to be coming to blows sooner or later. I'm just glad I was there to get in on it." His eyes crinkled in the corners with his smile.

She laughed. Of course he was. The Brooks boys never backed down from a good ol' fashion fight. The brothers were always close. When one fought, they all fought.

Together.

They stood in silence for a second. Curiosity was in Wade's eyes, but he held back on the questions she was sure he had for her.

Maddy pulled open the glass door and snagged a gallon of milk. She needed to move fast before Tyler found her.

"Again, thank you." She placed the milk in her cart.

"Hey, Mom!" Tyler yelled.

Maddy stiffened. *Shit.* She turned with a smile to see her boy bounding toward her like the gates of Hell had opened up behind him.

"How many times do I have to say, no running?" She put her hand on her hip and gave him her best *Mom means business* glare.

Maddy ignored the quick intake of breath from beside her.

"Umm…maybe a few times. I keep forgetting." Tyler gave her his infamous crooked grin.

She was hit with the strong resemblance to his father.

Why would God do this to her?

Tyler was a handsome boy, with his tan complexion and her dark hair, but his striking eyes were all his father's. Even the way his hair curled reminded her of him. His handy-dandy cowboy hat was on, giving him thr youthful cowboy look he strived for.

Her little boy was growing up to be the spitting image of the man who didn't even know he existed.

She was so screwed.

She'd have to go ahead and invest in a shotgun now to try to keep the future girlfriends away.

"You need to remember, young man," she scolded.

Wade's gaze was locked on the two of them. She couldn't meet his eyes, for if she did, she was sure she'd spill the beans.

"You could hurt someone. Or, better yet, knock something over."

"Mom, can I get both of these?" Tyler asked, ignoring her voice of reason.

It was then she saw he had two boxes of sugary cereal in his hands.

Frustrated, he glanced at both of them. "I couldn't decide."

She blew out a sigh and mentally calculated how much she had left in her checking account. She hated telling Tyler no, but she had no choice. They were on a strict budget for a few more months. With her online schooling costs and the move, her funds were practically depleted.

"No, baby. We can only get one." Her heart practically broke in two as she watched the light dim in Tyler's eyes.

He stood tall, his gaze flickering between the two before he finally chose.

"This one," he said. He placed the box in the cart and put the other one on a nearby shelf.

One day she'd be able to let him get two boxes of cereal. He deserved everything. He was such a good little boy. He never complained. Most kids would have probably thrown a temper tantrum, but not her boy. She'd always been honest with him, that with it just being her, they had to be careful about the amount of money they spent. She had started a nest egg once he was born for college. She was determined her son would make something of himself.

Tyler returned next to the cart. He took his first good look at Wade, and his eyes grew wide.

"Hey, mister, are you a cowboy?" Tyler's mouth hung open. Curiosity and excitement burned in his eyes. He was always rendered starstruck when he got to meet a cowboy, and today was no different.

Wade burst out laughing. He wore the standard flannel shirt, jeans, boots, and large belt buckle. Everything a cowboy needed, except a Stetson.

"Yes, sir. Howdy, lil' fella. I'm Wade Brooks." Wade held out his hand to Tyler.

Maddy could have sworn Tyler's chest puffed up a little. He stepped forward and took Wade's hand.

"I'm Tyler King," Tyler announced with pride.

"Wow, that's a strong grip you have there," Wade said dramatically.

Maddy bit back a snort.

"Thanks." Tyler backed away and hooked his thumb in his belt loop.

"Your dad teach you how to shake like that?" Wade asked. His gaze flickered to Maddy before returning to Tyler.

She flinched at the question.

"No, sir. My daddy isn't around," Tyler responded, not missing a beat. "Momma said he's a cowboy. I want to be a cowboy like him when I grow up. They are tough, strong, and good, honest men."

"They certainly are," Wade agreed. He rubbed his hand along his jaw. "Have you ever ridden a horse before, Tyler?"

"Yes, sir." Tyler bounced back and forth. "I love horses. We don't have any, but when I grow up, I'm getting me a bunch of them."

"Maddy, why don't you bring him out to the ranch. We have a program called Kiddie Camp. It's a great program for the youth. It teaches them ranching life, riding, camping, fishing, and every other skill we can bestow upon the new generation."

Tyler's eyes grew wider as he held on to every word that came out of Wade's mouth.

Maddy shook her head. There was no way she was stepping foot back on Blazing Eagle ground. Nausea filled her stomach at the thought of even putting one foot on the Brookses family land. The memories of the last time she was there were still present. She had never forgotten that day.

"Please, Mom? That would be so cool." Tyler turned to her with his pleading eyes.

Dammit. Her son was too smart for his own britches. He knew that look worked on her when he really wanted something.

Camps like that were expensive. She'd researched them before, wanting to give her son all of what Wade described. If Tyler wanted to grow up and be a rancher and a cowboy, then she wanted to help support his dream. But the financial side of it kept her from being able to do so.

She grew uncomfortable and embarrassed. She raised her arm and pushed her thick hair behind her ear. She caught sight of her hand trembling. She tucked it into her jean pocket, not wanting Wade to see it.

"I'm not sure I can afford something like that," she murmured. Again, her heart was sliced open. She had to tell her boy no to something he wanted so badly.

"We offer fair prices. Why don't you call and we'll work something out?" Wade reached into his back pocket and pulled out a business card. His hand paused in the air, waiting for her to take it.

"I'll think about it." She snatched the card and threw it inside her purse. "Come on, Tyler. We need to hurry home to put these groceries away. We have a big day planned."

Tyler waved to Wade. "Nice to meet you, Mr. Brooks."

She offered Wade a tight smile and grabbed their shopping cart. She guided it away from him and blew out a deep breath once they were no longer in his sight. Tyler silently walked beside her.

Thankfully, the checkout line wasn't too long. Tyler helped her load their purchases onto the conveyor belt for the cashier. He then moved to the end and loaded their bagged groceries into the cart. Her young boy was turning into such a young man. It would seem he always knew where he was needed.

Maddy sensed eyes on her. She glanced around and found Wade in the other line, looking at her. She turned away and focused on the total as the woman rang them up.

"Thank you," Maddy said to the cashier.

She took her receipt and pushed the cart out with Tyler skipping alongside her. They made it to her compact sedan that was barely holding on to life. Tyler helped her load the trunk.

Maddy caught sight of Wade getting into a fancy oversized pickup truck. Their eyes met. He gave her a nod and pulled off.

"Let's go, little boy," she said, slamming the trunk shut. "How about I make us some cookies?"

"Awesome!" Tyler ran and jumped into the back seat of the car.

She put the cart away in the store's parking lot collector and returned to her car.

She started it, and glimpsed in the rearview mirror at Tyler, with a wide grin on his face.

"What are you smiling for?" she asked, guiding the car around the lot and out onto the street.

"It was so cool to meet Mr. Brooks. He's a real-life cowboy." Tyler laughed. He turned his gaze toward the window with a smile still on his lips.

Maddy gripped the steering wheel tight to keep her hands from shaking. For almost nine years, she had been afraid of bringing Tyler to Shady Springs permanently. When they had come to visit, it had only been for a day or two, then they would go back to Colorado Springs. She'd always been afraid of running into any of the Brooks men. Even after all these years, Jonah's words still echoed in her head.

He can't afford to be brought down to your level.

She sniffed, holding back tears. She didn't want Tyler to see her this way. She blinked a few times to clear her vision.

"Mr. Brooks is nice," she murmured.

"How do you know him, Momma?" Tyler asked.

Maddy gulped. She hated lying to Tyler, so she kept her answer short and sweet.

"Well, growing up here in Shady Springs, everybody tends to know everyone," she replied. It wasn't a lie. The town was small enough that everyone did know everyone. Or, at least, knew the same people.

"Cool. I wonder what his ranch looks like?" Tyler mused. "I bet it's huge, with lots of horses and land."

Maddy didn't answer. The entire ride home, Tyler talked nonstop about the cowboy he'd met and going to ride horses.

Little did her son know, he'd just met one of his uncles.

MADDY WIPED OFF THE COUNTER, LOST IN HER thoughts. She and Tyler had a fun-filled day. Maddy didn't know where he got such energy from. She'd taken him to the park, as promised, where he'd ran for at least two hours straight with the neighborhood kids. They'd played soccer and other games. It did her heart good watching him make friends.

Unlike her, he was outgoing and eager to meet new people. She'd sat along the sidelines, watching him run and play while reading a book.

She rinsed off the rag and placed it to hang over the spout.

"Tyler King, are you done with your shower?" she yelled up the stairs.

"Yes, Mom!" he called back.

"Did you really wash? Do I need to come do the sniff check?" she joked. She folded her arms in front of her, waiting for his response. It was a long-running joke they had. Last year, she caught him sitting on the floor, playing with a few toys while the shower ran. The water hadn't touched his body once.

Ever since then, she threatened to come and sniff him to make sure he'd showered.

"Mom!" he shouted. The horror was evident in his voice.

She chuckled and moved around their small rented house, ensuring the locks on the doors were secured. In Colorado Springs, she had rented a modest, two-bedroom apartment that cost much more than what she was currently paying her new landlord. It was a reminder of why she had needed to move.

Arriving back in the living room, she quickly put all the pieces to her favorite game back in the box. Once Tyler was tucked into bed, she'd be able to pull out her laptop and do some of her homework.

After putting the game away, she turned out all the lights and headed upstairs. She knocked on Tyler's door.

"Come in," a muffled voice responded.

She pushed open the door and found Tyler sprawled across his bed, flipping through a book.

"Hey, buddy." She walked across the room and sat on the edge of the bed. She smiled and ruffled his hair. "What are you doing?"

Her eyes flickered to the book, and she saw it was one he'd borrowed from the library. It was a story about a boy and his horse.

"Reading," he murmured. He was so engrossed in the story, but it was getting late.

"Any good?" she asked playfully.

He glanced up at her with a crooked grin. "Yes. Nate and his horse, Stormy, are hilarious. Nate took Stormy on a train ride to go to his pa's house!"

They both shared a giggle. Maddy leaned over, and there was a picture of a little boy sitting on a train with his horse in the aisle.

"How did he get him on the train?" Maddy snickered.

"He just walked on." Tyler laughed, like a horse just walking on a passenger train was the norm.

"Okay, buddy. It's time for lights out." She stood from the bed.

"Aw, Mom. A few more pages?" Tyler looked hopeful.

"And if I did that, then you'd ask me for a few more, and then you'd be done with the book." She pulled the comforter from beneath him.

He climbed under and placed his book on the nightstand.

"You're right. I don't want the book to end just yet." Tyler laid back against his pillow with a big yawn.

Maddy covered him up and sat back on the edge of the bed, ensuring he was tucked entirely in.

"You are such a good son," she murmured, running a finger along his cheek.

"Mom," he groaned. He gave a dramatic roll of his eyes.

"Tyler King!" she scoffed.

"You're a good mom," he said quietly, his eyelashes fluttering against his cheeks.

Her heart filled with so much love for this young man. She didn't know what to say. He hated it when she got all mushy, but it was the mom in her wanting to make sure her little man knew he was loved.

"Thank you, baby. Your momma sure does try her best," she whispered. She leaned forward and pressed a soft kiss to his forehead. "Sleep tight."

Maddy stood from the bed and straightened the cover once more. Tyler's eyes were already closed, and his breathing was evening out. She flicked off the light and walked over to the door.

"Mom?" he called out.

"Yeah, babe?" She paused at the door and turned back to him. The room was basked in darkness. It took her eyes a second to adjust.

"Can you think about calling Mr. Wade? Maybe he can offer a good deal."

Maddy closed her eyes briefly before opening them again. "We'll see."

It wasn't a yes, and it wasn't a no. She'd think about it.

"Okay. Goodnight, Momma."

❧ 6 ☙

"**S**on of a bitch," Parker muttered. He glared at the broken fence before him, then scowled up at the sky. "Really?"

He blew out a deep sigh. He and some of the ranch hands had just fixed this portion about a month ago. A few heifers had escaped and were down at the creek. He never understood how the damn cows always cut through the fences. They had reinforced the hell out of it, but apparently, the stubborn cows still found their way through it.

"They really love that creek," he said.

The Blazing Eagle Ranch was a spread that hosted beautiful lakes, creeks, and gorgeous rolling hills. Parker was proud of the land that had been in his family for generations. He and his brothers would one day own it equally.

He sat quietly on his horse, Bandit, and gazed upon the Brookses' property. One day he hoped to have a wife and children to pass this down to. The ranch would be a beautiful place to raise children. He and his brothers had thrived here on this land. It made them who they were today.

With a grunt, Parker dismounted from Bandit. "Stay," he ordered.

The horse was well-trained. It would graze and stay in place until Parker called him. Bandit had been with him since he'd returned from the circuit. He had purchased him from a farmer who could no longer afford to keep him. Parker had worked with Bandit day and night to get him trained. The horse was intelligent, and had been eager to learn all the tricks that Parker had taught him.

Bandit also had a sweet tooth, so using sugar cubes as a positive reinforcement made the training extremely easy.

Parker walked over to the fence, and sure enough, it was pushed outward. He squinted over in the direction of the creek, taking in the few cattle grazing along the banks.

Stubborn cows.

He reached for the radio attached to his belt. He'd have one of his brothers bring the tools he needed to mend the fence once again.

"Parker, where are you?" a voice came through the speaker before he even had a chance to hit the button.

Shit. Wade must be psychic.

Parker immediately responded with his coordinates. "And bring supplies to fix this damn fence, too."

"Again?" Wade's incredulous voice responded.

"Yup."

"All right. I'm in the ATV. Be there in a few." Wade signed off.

Parker stepped through the opening and headed down toward the creek. He had to give it to the heifers. It was a beautiful area. If he'd had time, he'd bring up a few cold beers, relax by the big trees, and take in nature's beauty.

He pushed back his Stetson and tunneled a hand through his hair, then readjusted the hat. He leaned against a tree and watched the cows get out of the sun.

He glanced down at his hand. His fist was feeling slightly better. At least he was able to close it completely. Yesterday, he wasn't even able to bend his fingers. The skin was still discolored, and from experience, he knew it would get worse before it would look better.

Now that he was sober, he knew he shouldn't have gotten involved in Maddy's business. Derek was right, he would have handled the situation.

Parker didn't know what had come over him. He didn't know if it was the alcohol, or seeing another man put his hands on Maddy in a harmful way. All he knew was his feet carried him over to them, and he'd put an end to the situation.

Maddy King was back.

He couldn't believe it.

Seeing her had brought back so many feelings he thought he'd long buried years ago. It had taken him a while to get over her. When she left, she'd carried a piece of him with her.

The sound of an engine approaching broke through Parker's thoughts. He looked over his shoulder and caught sight of Wade in one of the ranch's ATVs.

Pushing Maddy from his mind, Parker walked back to the fence.

"Where have you been?" Parker asked. He hadn't seen his brother yesterday. It wasn't often they didn't see or talk to each other daily. He climbed back through the fence.

"I had some errands to take care of, and was running around town most of the day." Wade exited the vehicle. They gave each other a manly embrace, slapping each other on the back. "Don't tell me you missed me."

Parker rolled his eyes at him. That was one thing he loved about his two younger brothers, they always knew how to make him smile. Parker knew he could be a tough ass. Hell, look who their father was. He had tried to protect his siblings from their father. Jonah Brooks was a strict man who wanted his boys to grow up to be hard men like him.

But Grace Brooks ensured her boys had heart.

Jonah may have been an ornery son of a bitch, but Grace always had the last word.

"I wouldn't want to inflate your already oversized ego more than it is." Parker snorted.

They shared a chuckle and moved to the fence.

Wade let loose a whistle. "They were determined to get to the creek. It's a wonder they didn't get hurt." He assessed the damaged areas. Some sharp, jagged edges could have gouged a few of the cattle.

"Let's get the damn cows back on the other side of the fence before we fix it," Parker suggested. He called for Bandit, who lifted his head from grazing. The horse trotted over to him. "Good boy." Parker patted Bandit's neck.

He guided Bandit over to the opening carefully, ensuring he didn't get scratched. Once they were through, Parker hopped on Bandit and guided him down to the creek.

It took a little time, but they were finally able to get all the cattle back through the opening in the fence safely. Wade looked them over as best as he could before they continued moving on.

"Don't see no major injuries," Wade murmured.

"Good. No need to call the doc over," Parker muttered. Every time they had to call for Dr. Hutson to come for a visit, it cost a pretty penny, but he was worth it.

"Naw. We have tough cattle. They'll be fine." Wade grabbed the tools and supplies from the ATV.

Parker guided Bandit away from the fence to allow them room to work.

"We need for them to stay on the right side of the fence." Parker sighed, then winced, kneeling on the ground. Parker had difficulty bending his knee. He had seen multiple surgeons and doctors when he'd injured it. Damn bull had thrown him, and he hadn't even been quick enough to get out of the way. A thousand pounds of bull crushed his knee. After his last surgery and a stint of rehab, the damn thing still gave him problems.

He took the wire cutters out of the toolbox and paused. He glanced up at Wade, who just stood there, staring at him.

"You going to help, or are you just going to watch?" he snapped. He was not going to be the one working while his brother daydreamed.

"My bad," Wade muttered. He knelt beside Parker and pulled some gloves out of his back pocket.

They began working alongside each other, but Parker could tell something was eating at his brother.

"Spit it out already." Parker leaned back on his heels. There was no use in keeping shit bottled up. He pushed his hat back so he could see his brother. The sun was beaming down on them, and he squinted. "What's eating at you?"

Wade sighed and wiped his forehead with the back of his sleeve. He looked out at the land for a second before turning to Parker.

"I ran into Maddy at the grocery store yesterday."

"Okay." Parker shrugged and returned to fixing the fence. There were only two stores in town that had reasonably priced groceries. They were bound to run into each other sooner or later. "She lives here in Shady Springs, and I'm sure she needs to buy food."

"I'm not sure she's doing so well," Wade said gently.

Parker lifted his eyes to his brother. What the hell was that supposed to mean? Was she sick or something? Was that why she'd moved home?

"Are you going to continue, or do I need to play fifty questions?" Parker asked. His brothers sure could be dramatic.

Just tell the damn story.

"Financially, I mean," Wade clarified. "She looks great, but I think she's fallen on hard times."

Parker swallowed. It was no secret that the Kings had been a poor family. Everyone knew Robert King had squandered his money on booze and barely worked, leaving everything on Maddy and her mother.

Parker had never cared that she wasn't rich or from a prominent family. His family had more money than anyone in the county, but it didn't mean a thing. He'd been drawn to the pretty, shy young woman. Maddy had been nineteen when they'd started talking. She'd worked as a cashier at the local pharmacy, and he'd been twenty-two when he'd finally grown the balls to ask her out.

Parker had been on and off the circuits, just starting to make a name for himself. That spring, he'd finally approached her. Jonah Brooks had a problem with Maddy from the first time he'd found out Parker was dating her.

She's a gold digger.

You can do better than the town drunk's daughter.

She'll never make anything of herself.

His father's words still rang in Parker's ears.

There had been plenty of arguments between Parker and Jonah. His father had wanted him to find a good girl from one of the other larger ranching families.

But it was Maddy who had captivated and held Parker's attention. He was always drawn to her like a moth to a flame.

Just like he'd been the other night at the bar.

"She's a grown woman. I'm sure she's fine," he replied gruffly. He snagged the hammer and banged a few nails into the wood plank. Hopefully, this would last at least a few months.

"I know that, but she's got a kid."

Parker's breath was ripped from his lungs. He froze in place, the hammer hanging in his hands.

Maddy was someone's mother? He closed his eyes briefly before opening them.

Wade continued mending his part of the fence, apparently not seeing how his announcement affected Parker.

"The boy is as handsome as they come. He had on a worn little cowboy hat that has seen better days. Anyway, he came up to her and asked for two boxes of cereal. I could tell she was embarrassed that she had to tell him they could only get one."

Parker tightened his grip on the hammer. Where was the father? Why was she struggling alone?

"Anyway," Wade continued. "Her son is a cowboy fanatic. I gave her my card and told her about the Kiddie Camp. I even offered her a deal—"

"Give it to her for free," Parker interjected. He stared down at the grass, unable to look his brother in the eye. As much as Parker wanted to hate her for abandoning him, he didn't want her son to suffer. If they were indeed on hard times, and the kid wanted to be a cowboy, then they'd make damn sure he became one.

Parker thought back to when he was a child. He'd had everything he could ever want. Horses, dogs, dirt bikes, four-wheelers, and all the open sky and land a young lad would need.

Wade paused and met Parker's gaze. "Yeah, sure. We can do that. I didn't get her number, but she has mine. If she calls, I'll offer them a scholarship."

———

Parker stood under the spray of the showerhead and let the hot water run down his weary body. He'd done more than his share of work, and he was paying for it. All day his mind had been on the conversation with his brother.

Maddy had a child.

A little boy.

Parker was sure he was probably the spitting image of his beautiful mother. Genes like hers would be a shame to waste. Parker couldn't help but wonder if that was the reason she'd moved back to Shady Springs.

Was it a relationship gone wrong?

Did the guy hit on her?

Wade had told him the boy introduced himself as a King, so that meant she wasn't married, but why didn't the boy have his father's last name?

Parker ran a trembling hand along his face. He grimaced at the shadow of a beard on his jawline. Parker was too tired to shave it off now. It would have to wait until tomorrow when he had more strength. At the moment, he was likely to slice part of his face off.

He had to go see her. He didn't know where she lived, but he knew where she worked.

Fuck.

He wasn't sure Derek would even let him in the damn bar.

Parker grabbed his soap and began washing up. There was no way he and Maddy could avoid each other. They could be adults and have a conversation to clear the air. He needed answers, and maybe it would allow him to move on.

He rinsed himself off and cut the water. He reached outside the shower and snagged his towel, wiping his body down before stepping out. Wrapping the towel around his waist, he walked into his bedroom.

Parker felt like a new man after washing all the dirt and grime from his body.

He headed toward his closet and went inside. He reached up on the top shelf and pulled down a small shoebox where he kept his personal items.

With the box in hand, he went back out into his bedroom and sat on the edge of his bed. He opened the lid carefully and shuffled through the contents. His fingers landed on what he was searching for.

He'd saved pictures of him and Maddy from when they were younger. He placed the box on the bed and lifted the photographs out. The first one was a snapshot of them at the county fair. Parker had paid for someone to take their picture. His lips lifted up in the corner at the goofy expressions on their faces as they posed.

That summer had been the best one of his life. He and Maddy had been inseparable. He moved to the next picture. It was a day he had taken her out, wanting to teach her the fine sport of catching fish. He'd laid back against a tree and promptly dozed off. Maddy, being the silly person she was, took a selfie with Parker asleep in the background.

For at least a week after that day, she didn't let him live it down. He'd fallen asleep on their date.

Parker chuckled, remembering getting teased by his brothers over it.

He flipped to the next one, and his smile faded. This one had been a taken on a memorable night. The night Maddy had given herself to him.

He'd been her first.

He swallowed hard, remembering the night. It had been one of the most amazing experiences of his life. Afterward, he'd just held Maddy in his arms. She'd taken a picture of them cuddled together. It was the night he'd realized he was falling in love with her.

Parker stared at the photo, running a finger along it. He'd always loved the contrast of her skin against his. She was a few shades darker than him, and he remembered vividly worshiping her that night.

Maddy King had been the most beautiful woman in all of Shady Springs, and she had been all his.

Where did it all go wrong? What happened to them?

He pushed a hand through his hair and put the photos back in the box. Through all the years, he couldn't bring himself to destroy the few pictures he had of them. It was like if he threw them away, he'd be trashing a part of his heart.

There was no use thinking of what could have happened, or what he'd done wrong. He had been honest with Maddy from the start about his bull riding and the travel. She'd understood—at least he thought she had. Finding her gone had ripped a hole in his heart. She had betrayed him. Her leaving him had left him bitter.

He could have gone after her, but he would admit his young pride had gotten in the way. Now that he was older, he knew he should have made her talk to him. Followed after her. Hunted her down until he got an explanation.

But he couldn't turn back the hands of time and ask for a do-over.

Parker placed the box on his nightstand and stood. It was late, and he had to get up early in the morning to start work. That four-thirty alarm would be going off soon. He tossed his towel on the chair in the corner and climbed into his bed, naked.

His cell phone rang. Parker sighed and grabbed it off the nightstand.

"Yeah," he answered, not looking at the screen.

"Yo, glad you're still up," Carson's said through the line. He was way too chipper for this time of night.

"What do you want?" Parker snapped. He bit back a

yawn and threw his arm over his face to block out the light.

"I just got confirmation that Doc can come tomorrow. He wants to check the pregnant heifers to measure their pregnancy. He had a cancellation and can move us up."

"Fine. What time did he say he'll be arriving?" Parker asked.

"Between six-thirty and seven," Carson replied.

That would be perfect. He could leave around lunchtime and see if he could catch Maddy at The Tipsy Cow.

"All right. That's fine. See you in the morning," Parker said. He wanted to cut whatever conversation his brother thought they were about to have short.

"Yup." Carson disconnected the call.

Parker put his phone back onto the charger, turned the light on the nightstand off, and lay back against his pillows. Tomorrow was going to be tough. They would have to round all the pregnant cows up in the same corral to make it easier on Doc to do his checks. This would help them plan for the birthings.

Parker tried to push Maddy from his mind. Everything made him think of her. All day, she'd filled his every thought.

Tomorrow, he'd go to her. Get her to talk with him so they could clear the air. Maybe one day they could be cordial with each other. She could let her son attend

The Blazing Eagle's Kiddie Camp. It would be an excellent opportunity for a young man if he didn't have a male role model in his life.

Parker stared at the ceiling until his eyes drooped. A yawn hit him. He pulled the blankets up and turned over onto his side.

Maddy's smile came to mind.

He couldn't help thinking about her, so he gave in and allowed the fantasy version of Maddy to escort him into his dreams.

❧ 7 ☙

"It's such a beautiful day outside," Tod announced. He leaned against the counter and stared out the window.

"Get back to work, lazy," Maddy ordered playfully, slapping his arm as she brushed past him.

"How can I work when I know it looks like that out there?" He pointed outside.

Maddy sighed. She felt the same. Who wanted to work inside on a beautiful day like this?

"Well, a bright, beautiful sunny day doesn't pay the bills," she remarked. Today she was able to work the early shift at The Tipsy Cow. They had a fantastic lunch menu that attracted a nice crowd during the day, and it allowed her to pick up some extra money.

"That's the truth." He snorted.

Maddy moved to the sink and washed out the glasses that had been left. A few women had stopped in for lunch and had a glass of wine with their meals. She loved working the day shift. She got to meet interesting people. Not that night wasn't fun, it was. But at least during the day, everyone was sober and just needing company.

Best of all, it allowed her to be home in the evenings with Tyler.

"Fine. I guess I'll go act like I'm working," Tod said dramatically. "I'm going in the back to do some inventory."

"I can handle out here." She looked up, and there was a steady lunch rush.

Deb and the other servers were smiling and interacting with the customers.

She dried the glasses, remembering she would have to register Tyler for school. This fall, he would be starting at his new school, and they were both excited about his latest adventure. She was going to speak to Jerry to see if she could pick up more of the day shifts once school started. If not, then it was a good thing she lived close to her mother, where Tyler could go after school while she worked.

The sound of a chair scraping snagged her attention.

"Hey, Mike," she greeted the newcomer.

Mike was one of the local mail carriers who came in a few times a week for lunch. She'd only been working at The Tipsy Cow for a few weeks, and she was already starting to know the regulars on both shifts.

"Hello, Maddy. How are you?" He offered a grin. He set his hat on the table, revealing a dark mop of hair that was sprinkled with a few strands of gray.

"I'm doing well. What can I get you today?" Maddy asked, resting against the counter.

She pushed the lunch menu toward him, but he shook his head.

"My usual. BLT, chips, and a Coke."

"It looks like you've had one hell of a day. Want me to slip some rum into that Coke?"

He barked out a laugh and sifted his fingers through his hair. "I wish. I'm just on my lunch, but I may take you up on that once I finish my shift."

"You let me know. I'm here until after a happy hour." She tossed him a wink and walked back to the kitchen to place his order. Returning, she grabbed a frosted glass, dropped in some ice, filled it up with Coke, and placed it in front of him. "Rough day?"

"Yeah, you can say that," he muttered. He took a sip of his drink before settling back in his chair. "Got chased by a dog. Old man Wilson pulled a shotgun out on me."

"What?" she gasped.

"Someone needs to put the man in a home before he hurts someone. I was taking a package up to the house and needed a signature. Get to the door, and there he is, standing with a gun in my face."

"Oh my goodness. What did you do?" She leaned in, totally engrossed in his story.

"He yelled for me to get off his property. I swear that man doesn't know anyone. I called the sheriff's department, and they came."

"Were you able to deliver his package?" she inquired.

"Yeah. After the sheriff came out there and talked the old bat down, he signed for it." Mike took another sip of his drink.

She shook her head. "That's crazy. You sure you don't want any rum? I won't tell anyone," she teased.

Mike laughed and raised his glass. "This is good enough."

"BLT up!" Ryan, the cook, shouted from the window.

"That's you. Be right back." She pushed off the counter and made her way over to the pickup window. Mike's food was sitting there waiting for her. "Thanks, Ryan."

Ryan nodded. "Anytime, Maddy."

Maddy turned around with Mike's plate in hand and ambled back to the bar. Her gaze landed on a newcomer sitting at the edge of the bar. She stumbled and almost dropped the plate to the floor.

Parker.

His gaze was locked on her. She swallowed hard and made her way to Mike with a smile.

"Here you go," she announced. She placed his plate in front of him, handed him a few extra napkins, and topped off his Coke. "Need anything else?" she asked. She hoped he would to delay her greeting her new customer.

"I think that's all I need, Maddy. Thanks." He smiled and popped a few chips into his mouth.

"Holler if you need anything." She nervously wiped her hands on her apron.

Parker's attention was still on her. She smoothed down her hair and walked to him. It was a shame how good he looked. His infamous Stetson was low on his head. As she neared him, she was hit with the realization of how much bigger he was. Broad shoulders, large hands. Memories of his hands on her skin took her breath away.

Down, girl.

He didn't want you in the past, doubt he'd want you now.

Maddy had dated over the years. She'd even had a steady boyfriend once, but no one could ever live up to her expectations. She'd always had to be careful. She was a single mother with a child who was the top priority in her life.

Maddy had never wanted to be one of those moms who paraded men around her child. When she'd dated Luke, it had taken her months before she introduced him to Tyler. He had been kind to him, and her son had liked him. But things just hadn't worked out. By the second year, they both realized they'd be better off going their separate ways. There wasn't any drama, and it was an amicable split.

"Hi, Parker." She cleared her throat. "I'm surprised security let you back in here."

Parker's lip curved up in a brief smile. "I promised them I wouldn't be drinking, and only wanted lunch."

"What can I get you?" she asked softly.

He coughed and glanced around before settling his steel-gray eyes back on her.

"I'll have the special and a Coke." His voice was low, and it sent a shiver of arousal through her.

How was it after all these years, he could still cause the same reaction? She jerked her head in a nod and spun around.

"Maddy girl."

She froze in place. That had been his nickname for her. She had always been putty in his hands when he'd whispered it into her ear.

She looked back at him over her shoulder.

"We need to talk."

Without saying a word, she scurried to the kitchen and placed his order. She dreaded going back out there.

She stood by the door and breathed in deeply. Her heart raced. What did they have to talk about? It had almost been ten years.

Maybe moving to Shady Springs had been a mistake.

Maddy stood to her full height. She had to dig deep for bravery. There was no way he was going to run her out of town again. She had Tyler to think about, and right now, it was best they stay in Shady Springs.

She pushed open the door and walked back out to the bar. She grabbed a frosty glass, just as she had done for Mike. She took the Coke over to Parker and set it down in front of him.

"Thanks for the other night," she said.

He stared at her. "Billy had it coming."

She fought the urge to fidget.

"Well, thanks anyway." She shrugged.

"You look good."

She flushed and pushed her hair behind her ear. "Look, I don't think we have anything to talk about. I wanted to thank you and your brothers for coming to my rescue, but that's—"

"You know we do, Maddy girl. There's unfinished business between you and me," he said, cutting her off.

She glanced away from him and checked on Mike, who was busy eating his sandwich and watching the news on the television.

"I hear you got a kid," Parker said.

Her head flew around. She gripped her apron tight in her hands.

"Yeah, so?"

"Who's the father? Why isn't he here with y'all?" he asked. His eyes hardened at his own questions.

"That's none of your business." Her heart was racing so fast, it was a wonder she didn't pass out. Tyler was hers. She'd done what was asked of her. She left Parker alone so he could do something with his life. Well, she may not be wealthy or traveled all over the United States, but she'd done one good thing in her life.

She raised her little boy, alone.

There was no way she was going to let anyone take him from her. She'd fight them tooth and nail.

"Wade tells me your son wants to be a cowboy."

She folded her arms in front of her. Apparently, the middle Brooks brother liked to gossip.

"Yeah, and?"

"Give Wade a call and enroll him in Kiddie Camp. He'll love it."

She shook her head. "I can't afford it."

This was a mistake, coming over to serve Parker. She'd go find Tod and switch with him. He could watch the bar, and she could do inventory.

Parker was asking too many questions about her life. She had to leave.

"We'll give it to you for free. No charge," Parker said gently.

"I don't want your handouts," she snapped, narrowing her eyes at him.

Was that what he thought of her? Poor Maddy can't afford something good for her kid? Well, she may not have money like the Brookses, but she did have pride. Even with all the hardships she had to deal with as a kid, watching her father fail her and her mother, they never asked for help. As soon as she was old enough to get a job, she did so she could help keep the lights on in the house and food on the table. She'd held down a job since she was fifteen years old. She'd supported her and Tyler ultimately all on her own, and she'd be damned if she would ask for help now.

Parker must have seen something in her eyes. He held up his hands with his palms facing her.

"Think of it as a scholarship." Parker softened his voice. "We offer them for kids whose parents can't afford the camp. Most families around these parts can't, so it's our way of giving back."

She winced and shook her head.

No, she wasn't going to take handouts. No matter how Parker sugarcoated it, they were doing it only because she couldn't do it on her own.

"I'm serious, Maddy girl. Bring him. He'll love it. There are kids his age who get to learn how to ride horses, rope cattle, and even go camping on the ranch."

She was weakening. Parker was tugging on her

heartstrings. It sounded terrific, and Tyler would go crazy if he could go. Her shoulders slumped.

"Fine, I'll call him," she whispered. As much as she didn't want to, she'd do anything for Tyler. He needed something like this. It was all he'd talked about the last couple days since they'd ran into Wade.

"Daily special's up!" Ryan's voice broke through the tense air.

Maddy turned and went back over to the pickup window. Parker's plate was waiting on her. She grabbed it and heard her stomach growl. The special for the day was country fried steak with a heaping of mashed potatoes and gravy.

If she ate something this substantial for lunch, it would go straight to her ass. She'd picked up some weight over the years and never had time to do anything about it. Every month she'd claim she would start working out, but always found an excuse to avoid doing so. She wasn't substantially overweight or anything. Her full breasts, wide hips, and rounded ass still drew men to her. She'd try to wear clothes that would keep them at bay, but it didn't matter. She could wear a burlap bag and she'd get hit on.

She walked Parker's plate to him and set it down on the counter before snagging some extra napkins for him.

"Anything else you need?" she asked. She glanced over at Mike, who signaled for his check.

"Maddy girl."

Parker's deep, baritone voice sent a shiver through her. He gently took her wrist. Her gaze flickered to his, and it took everything she had not to get lost in his eyes.

"We need to talk," he said. "You tell me when and where, and I'll be there."

She stared at him. How had she forgotten he was as stubborn as a mule?

"Shady Creek. Tomorrow at noon." She snatched her arm away from him and spun around. She walked over to Mike to drop off his check.

He immediately handed her cash.

"Keep the change." Mike gave her a smile and pushed up from his seat. "See you later."

"Thanks, Mike. Take care." She headed over to the register, ignoring Parker. She knew without looking that he was watching her.

Deep in her gut, she knew the meeting with him was going to be a big mistake.

But those damn eyes of his got to her.

She could never tell Parker Brooks no.

Not in the past, and apparently not in the present either.

———

PARKER SHUT THE DOOR TO HIS TRUCK. HE SETTLED in his chair and blew out a deep breath. Parker rattled Maddy. When he'd walked into The Tipsy Cow, she had been relaxed and smiling. The second their eyes met, a wall went up.

He didn't know what she was hiding or what spooked her, but he would get to the bottom of it.

Parker had taken a chance on going to the bar to see if she was there. He was relieved to see she was working. He'd given his brothers an excuse that he had an appointment in town so he could leave without being questioned.

They'd been dealing with the cattle, so he'd rushed home and cleaned up before driving up to see her. He didn't want to show up smelling like cattle and manure.

Just seeing her again had his heart thumping.

Time had indeed been kind to her. He hadn't been lying when he blurted out that she looked good. Damn, her curves had his tongue tied like a young lad trying to speak to his girl crush.

The fire that appeared in her eyes when he'd mentioned letting her boy come to camp for free displayed her inner momma bear. Parker had always known she would be a great mother. She hadn't had the best example, but Maddy was a one-of-a-kind girl.

There was nothing wrong with having pride, but she had to know that he and his brothers loved helping people. Their father hadn't instilled that in them, their mother had.

Parker wished his mother was here. She'd be so proud of the Kiddie Camp they'd started. Wade had dreamed up the idea when he'd come back from college. The minute he'd brought it up to Parker and Carson, they all jumped on board.

Parker hit the start button to turn on his vehicle. The engine roared to life. He put it in drive and pulled out of his parking spot and headed home. He didn't want to stay away too long, or his brothers may suspect something.

His cell phone rang. He glanced at the screen and cursed.

Carson.

He tapped the hands-free to answer. "Yeah?"

"When are you coming back?" Carson asked.

"I'm on my way. You and Wade can't handle the fort?" he joked.

"Of course we can, but since you are in charge of the hands, they wanted to discuss vacations."

"Shit, I forgot they asked to sit down to talk about coverage." Parker ran a hand along his face. He had been too caught up in seeing Maddy that he'd let the meeting slip.

The Blazing Eagle Ranch employed four full-time hands and hired out as needed for the busy months. Kam, Stan, Darnell, and Rashad were all good men who had been at the ranch for years. During the summer, it was easier to find coverage with the extra help around to allow them to take some time off. The winter months were a little bit harder when it was just the full-timers working.

"I'll let them know you're on the way."

"Thanks."

"So," Carson began.

Parker rolled his eyes at his brother's dramatic pause.

"That appointment in town. It didn't have anything to do with Maddy, did it?"

Parker cursed again. His brothers knew him all too well.

"That's none of your damn business," he growled.

"Well, I just got my answer." Carson chuckled. "See you when you get here."

The call disconnected. Parker tightened his grip on the steering wheel. Tomorrow he'd finally get answers on what had gone wrong between him and Maddy.

Maybe they could one day grow to be friends. She was a single mother, and her boy sounded like someone he'd like to get to know. He could help her, be a male role model for her son. From what he knew, he didn't really have one.

Wade had shared with him that the kid said his father wasn't around. Getting him to the camp would be best for him. He'd get to interact with other kids his age and be around cowboys who were good men. Parker thought back to all the ranchers and hands who were around when he was growing up. Aside from his father, some of the older hands had helped mold him into the man he was today.

Tomorrow's meeting with Maddy was going to be good. He had a gut feeling that everything would work itself out.

❀ 8 ❀

"I hear we have a record number of heifers pregnant," Jonah said. He leaned back in his chair and took a long drag from his cigarette.

"Yeah. Doc checked them, and we're going to have a decent birthing season." Parker played with his hat that rested on his knee. They were going to have to start making plans to ensure the ranch would be able to absorb the costs that were associated with new cattle to feed.

Even though his ma was dead and gone, he still refused to wear the hat in her house.

He glanced down at his phone to check the time.

"You got somewhere to go?" Jonah's raspy voice spoke up. He flickered his gaze to his father.

Jonah Brooks was a big, burly man who was aging. Looking at him was like gazing at a version of himself in the future. Jonah would still be considered handsome by all standards. It had always been his attitude and demeanor that turned most people away from him.

Since Parker had come home for good, he'd taken over some of the responsibilities, being the eldest son. Soon, Jonah would retire, and the ranch would pass to him and his brothers.

"I do, but not for a while," he replied. He refused to tell his father exactly where he was going. It was none of his business.

His father grunted before taking a pull on his cigarette. "This quarter we've done quite well. I'm sure we can give the boys a decent bonus for a job well done."

Parker nodded. His father was a shrewd business-man, but he always made sure he took care of his men who were loyal to the ranch. Reliable hands were hard to find, and if he wanted to keep them, he had to make sure they were paid their worth.

Jonah Brooks was many things, and an intelligent businessman was one of them. Parker had learned a lot from his father. He tried to ignore the parts of his father he didn't agree with, but when it came to busi-ness, he and his brothers paid close attention to Jonah when he spoke.

His father always said he'd made the ranch into what it was, but his boys would be responsible for making it better and continue the Brookses' legacy into the future. The technology was advancing, and that was where the younger generation would come into play to ensure the ranch continued to thrive. Wade and Carson were college boys, implementing the things they had learned there.

"The men will appreciate it." Parker shifted in his seat. "Carson is driving down to Amarillo to meet with the buyers from Lone Star Processing," he announced.

Carson had taken to meeting with potential buyers of their cattle. He had a way about him, wrestling deals like Parker had never seen. It had to have been the smarts he'd inherited from their father.

Lone Star Processing was a major meat processing company. They had been in business for almost fifty years, and a standard in the cattle business. They were significant distributors to high-end restaurants and grocery store chains. They also had a string of wholesale stores where consumers took the middleman out and went directly to them to buy meat.

A contract with them would be a big deal. If Carson could land an agreement with them, it would help with the growth of the ranch. Parker was confident Carson wouldn't have any issues closing this deal. Their cattle were grass-fed and offered some of the best cuts of meat around. Blazing Eagle Ranch had a reputation for producing excellent quality.

"Nice. Lone Star is a big opportunity for us. This could net us a decent profit. Carson's a chip off his old man's block." Jonah chuckled. He leaned forward and snuffed the butt in the overfilled ashtray on his desk. "With as good as The Blazing Eagle is doing, it's time y'all find some women to marry and start families of your own."

Parker leaned forward. He took his hat in his hands and rested his elbows on his knees. He was tired of hearing Jonah talk about them settling down. His father always reverted back to the same lecture at least every other month. They'd listened to this since they'd turned twenty-one. He and his brothers would do it when they all found the right women.

Just because Jonah married their mother at the age of twenty-two, he felt they all should have been married off by this time.

"This isn't the eighteen hundreds, Pa. My brothers and I will settle down when we are ready," Parker replied, using his father's words.

"Is that so?" Jonah reached in his breast pocket and took out his pack of cigarettes. He pulled another one out and snagged his lighter off the desk. Jonah lit it and tossed the box and lighter down. He took a long drag before settling his gray eyes on Parker.

"You sure you want to keep smoking?" Parker asked.

His father was a heavy chain-smoker. It seemed he always had a lit cigarette in his hand.

"Seeing how lung cancer took Mama from us."

Grace Brooks had never touched a cigarette in her

life. She had been diagnosed with cancer when Parker was twenty years old. A year later, they had buried her. His heart still hurt with the thought of losing her. It seemed like it was just yesterday she'd yelled at him for walking into the house and forgetting to remove his hat.

Parker and his brothers had never picked up the nasty habit that consumed their father. None of them would openly blame their father for contributing to their mother's cancer. Jonah had taken his wife's death harder than anyone. It didn't need to be said. The man had suffered enough watching his wife die.

Jonah knew the secondhand smoke had played a part in Grace's death. He was intelligent, but kept on lighting those damn cancer sticks.

"What for?" Jonah shrugged. His stubbornness was legendary. "Your mama is already gone, and I reckon I won't be around too much longer."

"There's nothing wrong with you, Pa," Parker muttered, running a hand through his hair.

His father was still as strong as an ox, and just as ornery as one. He'd probably outlive all of them.

Parker glanced down at his phone again, and saw he had an hour to get to the meeting place Maddy had set. "If we're done here, I have to go."

"What's putting a fire up under your tail, boy? You too good to spend some time with your father?" Jonah snapped.

Parker shook his head. "Just meeting up with an old friend."

"I heard that King gal was back in town."

Parker stiffened. "Yeah, so?"

His father took another drag from the cig before crushing it in the ashtray. "Don't take that tone with me, boy. You stay away from her. Find you a decent gal. I hear the Macon's daughter, Vivian, is visiting. She's around your age. Single. We need to make sure the next generation arrives so we can have them run this stead. The land is already willed to you boys and your heirs."

"I'm okay, Pa." Parker stood from his seat, ignoring his father's words. There was no way he would be approaching a woman just because his father felt her family was fit for him. "I won't be gone long. Wade's out working that new mare, and we got Carson and some of the hands moving that head of cattle from the northern sector over yonder like you asked."

Jonah, his eyes locked on Parker, nodded.

Parker spun around on his heel and stalked from the office. He left the house, seething. He tried to remain calm. Jonah Brooks may run the ranch, but he didn't run his sons' lives.

———

PARKER WASN'T SURE WHY HE WAS SO NERVOUS. HIS hands trembled. He gripped the steering wheel tight as he drove to Shady Creek. It had been a while since he'd been there. Back in the day, it had been a place where all the young folk hung out and partied. The sheriff was called out there a few times a week for all the underage drinking and rowdiness.

He'd taken Maddy there a few times to meet up with friends. Now, the kids had found somewhere else to go to loiter. The town had renovated the park and made it more family-friendly. There were plenty of riding trails, walking trails, playgrounds, and picnic areas where families could meet.

It was a popular area with the residents. Parker put on his blinker so he could turn onto the road that wound throughout the park. He headed toward the parking lot. He didn't see any car parked at first. Then it dawned on him that Maddy wouldn't be at the open area where people could gather. He continued along the road, going deeper into the park. The creek was home to a luscious forest that attracted both humans and animals. There was one secluded area that he and Maddy would always escape to.

He pressed his foot on the gas, taking the winding curves of the road quickly. He came to the small clearing a few minutes later. A little beat-up sedan sat in one of three parking spots.

It had to be Maddy's.

He pulled in beside the car and killed the engine to his truck. He got out, and his gaze landed on the trail.

Everything appeared the same as the years before. He walked the path until he came to a secluded clearing. It was intimate, and only known to a few people.

Maddy had a blanket spread out on the grass with a picnic basket sitting on the edge. She looked up from her phone. The air escaped him. She was more beautiful than he remembered. Seeing her away from the bar and out in nature was like a kick to the stomach.

"What's all this?" he asked gruffly.

"A peace offering," she quipped.

He raised his eyebrows. He moved toward Maddy and sat down opposite of her on the blanket.

"I didn't know we were at war."

His eyes greedily took her in. The sun's rays shined down on her, highlighting her soft brown skin. Her tank top and cut-off shorts had his mouth watering. His dick had definitely taken notice and grew stiff. Her bare legs were smooth and the skin flawless. Memories of the legs wrapped around his waist sent a shudder rippling through him.

He glanced around, unsure why she'd bring them here. It was the place where they'd made love. He'd been her first, and she'd freely given herself to him almost in this exact spot. He turned his attention back to her and quietly watched her pull out the fixings for sandwiches and his favorite brand of chips. A few Cokes sat in a cooler behind the basket. It was a simple lunch.

It was just like his Maddy girl.

He paused. He'd called her that at The Tipsy Cow. He didn't know why he'd let his little term of endearment slip out.

She handed him a plate and watched him.

"You wanted to talk, so talk," Maddy said. She settled down on the blanket with her plate on her lap. She took a bite out of her sandwich, apparently waiting for him to start.

He raised his sandwich and took a bite. It was cold cuts with lettuce, tomato, and cheese, with a few slices of bacon. He groaned as the taste exploded on his tongue. It may have been just a sandwich, but dammit, Maddy did something amazing to it. He chewed and thought of what to say. He didn't know where to begin. Over the years, he had thought of all the things he'd say to her, but now that she was in front of him, he drew a blank.

"How's life been treating you?" he asked.

Dumb question, but at least it was a start.

She shrugged. "Not as well as yours."

"What is that supposed to mean?" His hand froze in the air with his sandwich. He looked down at it, wondering if she had an extra one in her basket.

She obviously saw the way he was contemplating the lunch and misinterpreted his look.

"Don't worry. I didn't poison it." Maddy chuckled. She put her plate down and wiped her hands on her napkin. "Life's been okay. It's hard to move on from someone when he's all over the television." She gave a dry laugh and reached into the cooler. She pulled out the two sodas and handed him one. She opened her Coke and took a sip. "I guess I should have moved farther away."

He was confused about why she'd left in the first place.

"So, if seeing me was so bad on television, why'd you move back?"

After swallowing, she cleared her throat. "My son. I needed help. I'm taking a couple of classes online. I needed a job that pays more money, and at least here, my mother can help babysit, and I don't have to pay her."

It seemed to be a good solid reason for her to come home. Parker understood, but something else was still bothering him. He, too, opened his Coke and sipped to quench his suddenly dry throat.

"Why isn't your boy's father helping you?" he asked.

What man would abandon his son?

"I don't want to talk about him." The walls were going back up.

Parker decided to leave that subject alone. He read her message loud and clear. Change the topic.

"Have you considered our offer for Kiddie Camp?" There. That was a safe. Wade had confirmed that she hadn't called him yet.

"I think so. I just haven't had time to call Wade yet.

My son would love it." She smiled. Her face lit up whenever she spoke of her son. "He loves horses so much. That was another reason I came home. You don't get this in the city."

She waved her hand around, and he knew she was talking about the town of Shady Springs. It was a safe community to raise children. The school was one the best in the state, there wasn't much crime, and it was a beautiful place to live.

They continued their meal in silence. Parker couldn't take his gaze off Maddy. His father's warning echoed in the back of his mind, but he pushed it aside.

"I'm still curious. Why did you really want to talk to me?" Maddy asked, meeting his gaze directly. "I doubt you wanted to talk about enrolling my son into the camp."

Parker took his hat off and sliced his fingers through his hair. He blew out a deep breath and replaced his cap back on his head.

"I don't know. I guess I needed to see you, talk with you. Get closure on what happened all those years ago."

Maddy grew still. She set her empty plate down on the blanket.

"What do you mean 'closure'?" Her chin tipped up slightly, and that fire he knew she kept hidden flared to life. Maddy was pissed. It didn't take a rocket scientist to figure this out. The way she narrowed her eyes on him and the change in her voice was the only evidence he needed.

He just didn't understand why she was so pissed. She was the one who'd abandoned him.

"Why did you leave? You knew I was going to be gone for a couple of competitions, then I was returning. I came back, and you just up and disappeared. Got a new number. That letter you left—"

"I never wrote you a letter." Her quiet words cut him off.

"What did you say?" he croaked. The color drained from his face. He couldn't have heard Maddy correctly. He remembered it just like yesterday. His father had come into the living room after Parker had returned from his trip. He handed Parker a white envelope with a letter signed by Maddy. His heart had been ripped from his chest. Out of anger, he'd thrown it in the fireplace, burning the letter. Now he wished he had saved it.

"I never wrote you a letter. I was too hurt by your leaving, and the fact you wanted to focus on your career that I had to go." She jumped up from her seat and stood, turning her back to him.

His heart was racing a mile a minute. He stared at Maddy and slowly stood. Her shoulders shook, and a hiccupped cry escaped her.

Well, if she didn't write him a letter, where did it come from?

He closed his eyes and willed his heart to slow down.

"Maddy girl." He cautiously approached her. He rested a hand on her shoulder.

She stiffened under his touch. He carefully turned her around to face him.

The sight of her tears almost brought him to his knees.

"Who told you that I wanted to focus on my career?" he asked. He already had a sinking feeling he knew who would be so cruel as to do something like that.

She sniffed and wiped the dampness from her face. "It doesn't matter. He was right. You got to make something of yourself. That's all that mattered, right?"

She moved to brush past him, but he snagged her arm.

Years of pent-up frustration, longing, and hatred for her flowed from him. Now that he was standing this close to her, desire, want, and need for her boiled over. He tugged her to him. Her body crashed into his, her full breasts crushed between them. He swooped down and covered her lips with his.

Fireworks went off.

A whimper escaped Maddy as she leaned into the kiss.

Parker was home.

9

Maddy threw herself into the kiss. The feel of Parker's mouth against hers fed the desire that burned for him. She stood on her tiptoes and slid her arms up his hardened chest. She entwined them together at the base of his neck. Maddy pressed closer to him. His kiss was addicting.

"Parker," she moaned.

Maddy quickly found herself flat on her back on top of the blanket. The grass beneath it created a plush, comfortable mattress. She reached up and pushed Parker's hat from his head, needing to feel his hair between her fingers. He braced himself over her. She spread her legs wide to allow him to settle into the valley of her thighs.

He commanded the kiss. His tongue swept inside

her mouth, coaxing her to duel with his. He angled his head and deepened the kiss.

Parker broke away from her, trailing hot kisses along her jawline down to her neck. She dove her fingers into his soft, silky curls. She'd never understood why he kept them hidden under his hat.

Her body grew hot with need.

It had been entirely too long since she'd been touched by a member of the opposite sex. Parker's large hands slid down her waist and disappeared underneath her tank top. The feeling of his calluses against her skin sent a shiver through her body.

Her hands went on an exploration of their own. Parker was complete muscle. Not the gym membership muscles, but the ones earned from hard, backbreaking labor on a ranch. She pushed his shirt up, wanting to feel his bare skin.

"Maddy girl," Parker murmured. He brought his face up to hers, holding her eyes. "Are you sure?"

"Yes, God. Please," she breathed.

She reached up and pulled his face down to hers. Their lips merged into a deep, passionate kiss. She poured all the years of frustration into this kiss.

Parker tore his lips from hers and sat back on his heels. He tugged his shirt over his head, revealing his chiseled chest and perfectly sculpted abdomen. Maddy's core clenched at the sight of him. He had a golden tan from all his years working out in the sun. She ached to touch him.

Taste him.

He leaned forward and reached for her shorts. His fingers flicked open the button while their eyes locked.

His hair fell forward on his forehead. Maddy reached up and pushed it away from his eyes. He undid her shorts and took them off of her.

She quickly discarded her tank and dropped it onto the ground next to her shorts.

Parker's eyes darkened as he took her in. She had been self-conscious about the shape of her body before, but now under Parker's assessment, she was proud of her curves.

"Damn, Maddy girl," he breathed. His hands roamed her body, starting at her thighs, then traveled up her soft tummy to her full breasts. "Your body is perfect," he whispered.

She smiled and shook her head. "Hardly."

She rested her hand on his shoulder and ran it down along his pectoral muscles.

"Don't try to tell me what I find beautiful," he growled. He leaned forward, pressing a hard kiss to Maddy's lips. His hand trailed up her stomach to the clasp nestled between her breasts.

In shock, she lay there.

With an attitude like that, he could have his way with her.

Parker opened the bra and freed her aching mounds. His quick intake of breath connected with her core. He slid the contraption off of her and tossed it over his shoulder.

"Beautiful," he murmured. He lowered his head and licked her beaded nipple.

She gasped, arching her back. Parker gripped her breast in his hand and sucked her nipple into his hot mouth.

She threaded her fingers into his hair and held him in place. A sexy growl escaped him as he moved to her other one. Her body writhed on the blanket while he took his time.

"Parker," she gasped.

He nipped at her bud, teasing her, as she stared at the bright-blue sky. It was a beautiful backdrop to what was transpiring between them.

She should have been mad at him, but she no longer had it in her heart. They both had been duped. They had missed years with each other because of the hatred someone else had in their heart.

Parker traveled lower, planting open kisses to her belly. He put himself at eye level with her core. He gripped her thigh in his hand and pressed soft kisses there.

The sight of his brown hair between her thighs was a fantasy she'd held dear to her heart for years. He was exactly where he belonged.

She was completely turned on and strung tight. She wasn't above begging to be put out of her misery.

"Your scent. I can still remember it," Parker whispered, dragging his tongue down the soft inner part of her thigh.

"Please," she whimpered.

Parker ran a finger against her damp panties and gave a deep chuckle.

"Is this all for me, Maddy girl?"

The way her name fell from his lips brought goose bumps to her skin.

"Yes," she hissed.

Parker trailed his finger near the outline of her labia. She didn't care what she looked like with her legs spread wide, her body writhing on the ground.

She needed Parker.

She needed to feel him inside her.

Parker slid her panties to the side, revealing her fully to him. Her body stiffened at the first touch of him on her bare skin.

"Look at this," he murmured.

She whimpered when he spread her labia apart. His tongue ran along the same path and landed on her clit.

A deep moan escaped her. She tightened her fingers in Parker's hair as he devoured her. She ground her hips against him, her body moving of its own accord.

He pulled back and yanked her panties down her

legs. He pushed her legs wide open and returned back to her.

He introduced a finger inside her slippery core. She released a curse when he drew it out, only to add another one.

"I need to feel you inside of me," she begged, tugging on his hair.

Parker promptly ignored her, fucking her with his hand while teasing her swollen nub with his tongue.

She grew flushed. Even though she was naked outside on a perfect day with a nice gentle breeze, her body was overheating.

Only Parker could solve her problem.

"Not yet," he muttered.

Maddy moved her hips to the rhythm that he set. Her orgasm was building. It would seem even ten years later, Parker still knew how to take her to the brink of heaven.

"Parker," she chanted his name repeatedly. She turned herself over to him. Her muscles tensed while she teetered on the edge.

Parker thrust his fingers in deep and twisted them around, finding the right spot. Her body detonated, her back arching into the air again. A cry broke from her as she rode the waves of her orgasm. She flopped down onto the ground, spent.

A primal growl escaped Parker. His eyes were dark

when his gaze trailed along her body. He quickly removed his boots and jeans.

Dammit, the man still didn't wear underwear.

His massive cock sprang free, captivating her. It was the most perfect dick she'd ever seen.

He covered her body, and with one swift thrust, he sank deep inside her.

He grunted, holding still to allow her to adjust to his invasion.

Maddy opened her eyes and found Parker staring down at her.

He leaned down and kissed her. She tasted the slight hint of herself on his tongue.

He broke the kiss and nestled his face into the crook of her neck. Maddy wrapped her legs around his waist.

Parker pulled back and slammed into her, eliciting a gasp from her.

"Maddy girl," he moaned.

Her core clenched around him while he controlled the rhythm. He was tenderly fucking her. The feeling of him inside her was glorious. He was a large man and stretched her out. She knew he was trying not to hurt her, but she wanted more.

"Parker," she gasped.

It was as if he sensed what she needed. His strokes became harder, faster.

Maddy met his thrusts with her own, driven by his moans of pleasure. Hearing a man so vocal during love-making was a complete turn-on.

At the moment, it was just her and Parker.

No one to interfere with what was between the two of them.

They were in their own little secluded world.

He lifted her leg higher, opening her more to him. He changed his angle, prompting a cry from her. She dug her nails into his biceps with every deep thrust. She cried out, uncaring if anyone passing by heard them.

Parker's hoarse groans mixed with hers. He threw his head back, the muscles in his neck bunched tight.

"Maddy girl. I need you to come with me, baby." His voice was strangled. He slid a hand between them, his fingers finding her slick nub.

Her lips parted at the feeling of him rubbing her clit. Her head tilted back when she reached her climax again. Her muscles tensed, and she dug her nails into Parker again, this time not letting go.

Her hips ground against his. He thrust harder and harder until he reached his release. His shout echoed through the air as he poured himself into her.

They gripped each other tight, floating down from their orgasms.

Collapsing on top of her, she wrapped her arms around him, not wanting to let him go.

"I'm too heavy for you," he muttered, his lips brushing her ear. He tried to push up and off of her, but she held him close.

"Please, don't move," she whispered. She basked in the feel of Parker's muscular body covering hers. He was still buried inside her, and she didn't want to break their connection. Too many nights she had dreamt of being with Parker. She had written off being with him ever again. How would that happen if he didn't want her?

The warmth of his body comforted her. His scent was one that she would only attribute to Parker. It was a slight musk with a sandalwood smell that she loved.

If she could, she would stay right here forever.

She softly ran her fingertips along his muscular back. He'd bulked up and filled out over the years. Parker Brooks had been cute and handsome when they were younger. He'd had defined muscles that she used to ogle whenever she got the chance. She had been infatuated with the then twenty-two-year-old Parker. The older Parker was scorching hot, and sexy as all sin.

He lifted his head and stared into her eyes. He rested on his elbows, taking some of his weight off of her. He ran a finger over her cheeks and trailed it to her lips, studying her as if trying to memorize her features.

Looking up at him, it finally dawned on her.

There was no question now why no other man in her past could ever live up to the high expectations she had set. She'd always used Tyler as a crutch when it came to men and relationships. She always put her son as the top priority. But now she knew the actual reason why she was never satisfied with anyone else.

She was still in love with Parker Brooks.

arked sighed, loving the feel of Maddy nestled into the crook of his arm. Her naked form pressed against him had his cock stiffening again. He tried to will his dick to calm down, not wanting to scare Maddy away.

He ran a hand along her arm as they stared at the sky. It was bright blue with a few clouds.

He blew out a deep breath, knowing they needed to finish their conversation.

"It was my father, wasn't it?" he murmured.

Her muscles tensed under his touch. She didn't have to say a word for him to know the answer.

"It's in the past." She sniffed. She sat up with her dark hair falling around her shoulders.

Parker was mesmerized by the sight of her warm brown skin. Her chocolate-colored areola begged for his tongue again. He turned to her and leaned up on his elbow.

"What are you doing?" he asked.

"My clothes." She stood and began wrestling with her clothes.

"What's wrong?" He grew concerned as he watched her.

She hiccupped, and he realized she was crying. He stood and snagged his jeans. He threw them on and moved to her.

He rested his hands on her shoulders and pulled her back to him. "Maddy girl, tell me what's wrong?"

She spun around. Her eyes were red, puffy, and tears streaked her cheeks. She pushed her hair from her face and closed her eyes briefly. Her lips trembled while she fought to keep from crying.

"It's all his fault," she cried out. The tears ran freely down her face. She paced back and forth, running her hand through her hair. "I should have gone to you. I shouldn't have listened to him. He's a vile old man—just evil. How could he have done something like that?" Sobs racked her body. She paused and held a hand to her mouth.

"I'm going to have a talk with my father. What he did was ludicrous." He walked to her and gripped her shoulders tight. He tipped her chin up to force her to look him in the eye. "After all these years, we're here together. Fate brought you back to me. Nothing can keep us from each other. He can't intervene in our lives anymore, Maddy girl."

That, he would promise her. He and his old man were due to have one hell of a chat. Parker couldn't even explain how pissed off he was at his father. All these years, Parker had hated Maddy for leaving him.

He wrapped his arms around her. She leaned against him while she continued to cry.

He rubbed her hair and whispered sweet nothings into her ear to try to calm her down. He wanted to kick his own ass. He knew how his father was, and shouldn't have believed anything Jonah Brooks said. He should have demanded someone give him her contact information so he could confront her face-to-face on why she'd ghosted him.

Instead, his damn pride had got in the way, and he'd thrown himself into his career.

Parker tried to control the rage he felt in his chest. All these years they'd missed, all because his father didn't want him to be with her.

Jonah Brooks had gone too far.

He'd butted into Parker's life and cost him someone who had been very precious to him. As soon as he tended to Maddy, he was going back to the ranch to have a firm conversation with his father.

All of this animosity against Maddy because she wasn't from a well-to-do family ended today.

"Maddy girl, let's start over. You and me. How about that?" he asked.

She pulled back and stared up at him with her big brown eyes. He reached up and wiped the wetness from her cheeks. Her eyes were swollen and red, but she was still the most beautiful woman he'd ever known.

"That's going to be really hard, Parker," she replied.

He frowned, confused as to what she meant. He didn't think she was seeing anyone else. He wasn't at the moment. What would be so hard about them just starting over?

Maddy peeled herself away from him. She took a step away from him and wrapped her arms around her middle. She looked so alone and broken.

"Parker, I came to your house on that day you were to leave just like we had planned." She rubbed a hand along her face before turning her attention back to him.

He remembered the day. He had woken up late, and when he came down the stairs and got ready, she never showed up. He had called her and left her a message, but she'd never called him back.

Dread filled his stomach while he watched her compose herself.

"I knocked on the door, and your father came out onto the porch. He told me you had already left. He convinced me you were better off without me." She angrily wiped tears from her face with the back of her hand. "That man had me convinced I would hold you back from your dreams and your career. I knew how much bull riding meant to you, and it was your passion. To be successful, you would need to work hard to make a name for yourself."

She blew out a deep breath and stood still.

Parker rummaged through his hair. He bent down and snagged his shirt and put it on. His anger was rising even higher. He would never be able to look at his father the same. He knew Jonah Brooks could be malicious and cruel, but this was even below his father's norm.

"Just like you said, it's in the past. It'll be okay." He moved to her, trying to take her back into his arms, but she stepped away from him.

"It's not," she cried out. "I made the worst mistake of my life."

"What are you talking about?" he asked, exasperated. They could forget the past, start over today, and see where this thing between them would go. They were perfect together. Just one time was not going to be enough. He needed more of Maddy. Her body belonged to him. The way she'd responded to his touch was proof enough.

Maddy covered her face with her hands and took a few deep breaths. Parker stood in front of her, waiting. She moved her hands and stared up at him. The pain in her face took his breath away.

"Parker, I had planned to tell you the day you left that I was pregnant."

The blood drained from his face. He took a step back, as if he had been hit in the solar plexus with a two-by-four.

He couldn't have heard her right.

"Pregnant?" he croaked. "Pregnant with my baby?" He closed his eyes, picturing a timid Maddy trying to stand up to his father. He should have been there. They should have made other plans that weren't at the ranch. He knew his father had it out for Maddy. Jonah never bit his tongue about the daughter of the town's drunk.

Parker should have protected her better.

It was almost as much his fault as it was Jonah's.

"What...what happened to the baby?" It just about choked him to ask. They had created a life together. His heart was pounding. Did she give the baby up for adoption? Did she...terminate? He swallowed hard.

He'd kill him.

Parker had never wanted to harm his father before today.

"That baby is a nine-year-old little boy who wants to be a cowboy when he grows up." She finally smiled through her tears.

A son.

He had a son.

One who wanted to be a cowboy like his father. Parker blinked a few times. He had a boy.

Holy fuck.

He was a father.

"What's his name?" He was pretty sure he was told before, but he hadn't really paid attention. When Wade had shared with him she'd had a kid, he hadn't even asked for a name. He was too busy thinking of himself and what she'd done to him.

Now he was dying to know.

"Tyler," she said hesitantly. She visibly swallowed hard and glanced away for a second. "Tyler King."

Parker grimaced. Hell, his boy didn't even have his last name. Well, what did he expect? He hadn't been there.

He ran a hand along his face. Maddy obviously saw the reaction.

"When he was born, I had to leave the line where the father's name goes blank. You weren't there to sign his birth certificate," she whispered.

It was like receiving a cold splash of water to his face. She'd had to bear his child alone. While he was off riding bulls, drinking, and living life, she had to raise a son.

"Can I meet him?" he asked. Parker didn't know much about children, only that he wanted some one day. He hung around with the kids that attended Kiddie Camp each summer, but Wade ran that. Parker's brother was like a kid whisperer. They all looked up to him and followed him anywhere. "What does he know about me? Have you even told him about me?"

The questions poured out of him. Did the kid even know he had a father who was alive and didn't know about him? If the kid was a true Brooks, he was curious by nature. Parker and his brothers had gotten into plenty of trouble back in their youth due to their inquisitive natures.

"I told him he had a father who was a cowboy, and one day he'd get to meet him." She rushed toward him and stopped directly in front of him. "I swear I've never spoken ill about you, Parker. No matter what I thought you had done to me, I could never take your name in vain."

He finally succeeded in tugging her to him. He tipped her chin up so he could look her in the eyes. She didn't know it, but she'd just given him one of the best gifts he could have ever asked for.

"Words can't express how sorry I am. You shouldn't have had to raise Tyler by yourself. I let my pride get in the way. I should have run after you. I'm so sorry, Maddy girl."

He vowed that moment he would not rest until he'd fixed this wrong.

"I'm sorry I let your father influence me. I should have known better, but I was vulnerable and thought I was doing what was best. A baby and a girlfriend would have held you—"

Parker placed a finger on her lips to silence her.

"I would have made it work, for you and our baby."

Fresh tears fell from her eyes. Parker leaned down and captured her lips with his in a sweet, soft kiss.

He pulled back, but was unable to resist pressing one more kiss to her plump lips. "When can I meet him?"

The excitement grew inside his chest. He couldn't wait to meet his son. There was so much he could teach the little guy.

Maddy smiled and glanced down at her watch. "He and my mother went to the movies. How about I grab him when they get back, and you can come over to our house for dinner?"

That would give him a few hours to figure out what to say to Tyler. How would he explain his absence?

"That sounds like a plan." It was a smart one. It would allow them to meet on familiar ground for the kid.

"I'll cook his favorite meal. Is six okay?" Maddy asked, resting her hand on his chest.

Parker nodded and gathered her to him. He leaned down and rested his forehead on hers.

"Everything is going to be okay, Maddy girl. I promise."

———

Maddy folded the blanket while Parker packed the basket with the leftovers, quickly cleaning up their area. She hated to leave him, even if only for a few hours. They had so much to catch up on.

He held out his hand for her. "Come on. I'll walk you to your car."

She slid her smaller one into his and offered a small smile.

"You and that hat."

He glanced over at her. "You need one. No self-respecting mother of a cowboy should walk around without one."

"Tyler would go crazy if I had one." She giggled. She leaned into him as they walked through the woods.

Finally, she felt at peace. Like a weight had been lifted from her shoulders now that her secret was out in the open. The next step was introducing Tyler to Parker.

She immediately began thinking whether she had everything she needed to make his favorite meal—lasagna. She needed fixings for a salad since Parker was coming over. Tyler refused to eat anything that looked like rabbit food, as he would say, so she rarely bought a bag of lettuce because it wilted and went bad before she could finish it all.

She made a mental note of everything she would need from the store. She'd stop by and splurge a little on her men.

Her men.

She didn't know what the future held for them, but she had a funny feeling Parker wasn't going anywhere.

"What type of toys does he play with?" Parker asked.

"The usual. Tyler loves remote control cars, anything that has to do with horses." She shrugged, trying to think of everything her son was in to. "He loves sports. Soccer and football are his favorite."

Parker chuckled. "Carson is going to love that."

Maddy had forgotten the Brooks brothers all played football in high school. With their size, it would have been a crime for them not to.

"You know, Carson played football in college."

"He did? I didn't know that." It was uncanny how similar Tyler was to his father and uncles. She guessed it was just the Brooks genes he'd inherited.

They continued on in comfortable silence. Maddy enjoyed the quietness around them. It was as if they both needed to absorb everything that had transpired over the last few hours.

They arrived at the edge of the trail that led to where their vehicles were parked. They walked over to Maddy's car. She pulled her keys from her purse and unlocked it so they could toss the items in the back seat.

Maddy turned around and stared up at Parker. She

reached up and brushed away a few pieces of grass that clung to his shirt.

His lips curved up in his crooked grin. His face totally transformed when he smiled. It was infectious. A silly grin spread across her face.

"So, six o'clock," he began. He trapped Maddy against the car with his hands on both sides of her.

"Yeah. Don't be late," Maddy teased.

"I won't be, darlin'." He thickened his country drawl. "Wild horses wouldn't be able to keep me away from you and our little boy."

"Good."

"We have so much time to make up for, Maddy girl." The smile on his face disappeared, and was replaced by a concerned look.

Her stomach clenched every time he said her nickname. Ten years later, and she still fell for it.

"We do, but we shouldn't rush it. Especially not with Tyler. I just don't know how he's going to react," she admitted.

"I have all the time in the world. I'm a patient man, and whatever it takes, I'll do it for Tyler."

She nodded and leaned her forehead against his chest. It felt good to be in his arms again. She sent up a quick prayer that everything would work out like he promised.

Tyler was a tough kid. He'd be fine. She knew deep down that he was just waiting for the day his father rode into town on his horse. Today, he would finally get his wish.

"I gotta go," she murmured, lifting her head.

He bent down and pressed his lips to hers. Her mouth immediately opened, granting his tongue entrance. The kiss turned heated. His hands cupped her bottom and brought her flush against him.

A horn blaring from a passing truck had them jumping apart.

Maddy laughed, while Parker cursed the driver.

"Text me your address," he said as he opened the driver's side door to her car.

They pulled out their phones and exchanged numbers. She sent him a quick message with her address.

"Done." She stood on her toes and pressed a kiss to his chin before sliding into the car.

Parker closed the door and backed away from the vehicle. She put the key in the ignition and turned it. The engine roared to life. She gave him a little wave and backed out of the spot before guiding the car onto the road.

A small smile remained on her lips.

Everything was going to be okay. Maddy was sure of it.

11

Maddy sat on her mother's porch and waited for her and Tyler to return. Now that she'd had time to think of everything that had happened today, an overwhelming sadness filled her heart.

She didn't know what she'd ever done to warrant such hatred from Jonah Brooks, but he was a mean old man who would one day pay for what he had done.

Maddy was a firm believer in karma, and she was going to come right back around and deal with the elder Brooks.

Maddy wasn't a person who hated anyone, but she had a strong dislike for the man. He had no conscience. Jonah couldn't. He went on with his life just fine while everything in hers and Parker's lives changed.

She was glad she was able to get everything off her chest with Parker. She understood that Jonah had played a significant part, but she and Parker could have gone to each other and talked. Cleared the air instead of allowing themselves to be manipulated by a man who never hid the fact that he hadn't wanted his son dating the daughter of the town drunk.

The air was clear now.

Tonight, Tyler would finally meet his father.

After leaving Parker, she had run home and jumped in the shower. She'd hated washing his scent from her body, because being back in his arms had been fantastic. It was like she had come home. Just remembering the feeling of him thrusting deep inside her had her clenching her thighs together.

She chuckled and fanned herself to cool down.

There was no other way to describe what she felt when she was with him earlier. All she knew was that it seemed right. Before arriving at her mother's home, she'd stopped by the store and purchased the few items she needed to make their dinner with some of her rainy-day funds. She wanted tonight to be perfect for Tyler and Parker.

Maddy caught sight of her mother's white sedan making its way down the street. She watched the car turn into the driveway.

She found herself nervous about telling her son that

he was going to meet his father. She knew Tyler. If she told him who he would be meeting now, he'd drive her crazy until Parker arrived at their home.

Her mother parked the vehicle in front of her garage door. The car shut off, and no sooner than Maddy could stand, Tyler came bounding out the back door.

"Mom!" he hollered. He slammed into her, wrapping his arms around her waist.

"Hey, baby. How was the movie?" she asked.

"It was cool. Nana fell asleep through parts of it." Tyler laughed.

She gave him another tight hug.

"Mom, you're squeezing me to death."

"I am not. I'm just loving on you," Maddy said. She released him and pointed to the house. "Run in and grab your stuff. We have to get home."

Myla walked around the car, observing them. "What's going on?" she asked.

Maddy watched Tyler jog up the stairs and disappear into the house before she turned back to her mother.

"I decided to finally introduce Tyler to his father tonight," she announced.

"It's about time." Myla snorted. She hoisted her purse up onto her shoulder and folded her arms in front of her chest.

Maddy stared at her mother in disbelief.

Unbelievable.

Myla never failed to amaze her. She'd never understood how a person could be so negative in life. Maddy used to blame it on her father. With as much stuff as he'd put Myla through, Maddy used to feel sorry for her.

But her father had been dead for years now. There was no reason for Myla to still be the same way.

"Mom, I've done my best with Tyler. I wish you would give me some credit. Everything I do is for that boy in there." Her chest was rising and falling fast. This was the first time Maddy had actually stuck up for herself to Myla. She usually just left and wasn't a confrontational woman. Look where'd that had gotten her in life.

Maddy King was done with people running all over her.

Myla stood a few from feet away from her with a shocked expression. Myla breathed out a deep sigh. She shook her head and met Maddy's gaze.

"You're right," Myla said.

Maddy took a step back and almost fell down on the stairs. She couldn't have heard her mother right. Those two words rarely came out of Myla King's mouth.

Myla's lips were pursed together in a thin line. It was uncommon for Myla to put on a display of emotion or show much affection.

"You are one of the strongest women I know," Myla

admitted. "I wouldn't have been able to do what you have done. Moving away, pregnant, to start over in a city where you don't know anyone was brave. I've watched you work hard for you and your son."

Maddy's mouth opened, but no sound came out.

Myla continued. "I'm so proud of the way you have raised that boy. He's respectful, he's kind, and has a big heart. I'm so thankful that you moved back to Shady Springs so that I can be a part of his life."

Maddy didn't know where they came from, but her tears were back and blurring her vision. Today must be the day for crying. She had thought she was all cried out when she was at the creek with Parker.

Myla stepped forward and wrapped her arms around Maddy. It was the second time that Myla had done such a thing in a short span of time. She couldn't even remember the last time she'd hugged her mother this much.

"Thank you," Maddy whispered. She closed her eyes tight and held on to her.

"I know I wasn't the best parent to you, but I did what I thought was best." Myla squeezed her hard. "Your father drained the life from me, but I shouldn't have let that affect our relationship, and I'm sorry."

Maddy returned the tight hug. There were years of pain that they'd both suffered in the house when her father was alive. He was never one to hit or beat them, but his words were sharper and harder than any fist could have been. Robert King had placed a wedge between mother and daughter.

Even after her father died, Maddy hadn't come around much. She'd taken Tyler to visit with her mother so he could get to know her. It was the only family they had, and even though their relationship was strained, it was better than nothing.

Maddy had always hoped that she and her mom would have a breakthrough. She wanted a better relationship with Myla.

Maybe today would be the push they needed in the right direction.

"What is the plan?" Myla asked. She wiped her cheeks, removing the evidence of tears that had streaked her face.

"I invited him over for dinner. I figured my house was the most familiar and comfortable for Tyler." Maddy tucked her hair behind her ear.

Myla nodded. "That's a good idea."

"I'm ready!" Tyler came flying out of the house. He jumped down the stairs and landed on his feet. His duffle bag was stuffed with his clothes and was only half zipped.

"Tell Nana bye," Maddy said. She took his bag from him so she could close it correctly.

"See you later, Nana." He gave Myla a hug.

She laughed and wrapped her arms around him tight. Maddy smiled, watching the two of them.

Moving back to Shady Springs appeared to not only be good for her and Tyler, but her mother, too. There was a lot that Maddy and Myla needed to work through, but this was a start. Maddy and her mom shared a look over Tyler's head.

"Have fun tonight." Myla kissed him on his forehead and let him go. "He's so tall. He's almost as tall as we are."

"Nana, I'm going to be super tall when I grow up," Tyler quipped.

"Okay, little man. We have to get the house organized and cleaned from top to bottom. We are having company coming over later today." She helped him into the car and got in. She glanced back at her mother, who was waving from the porch. She honked her horn and drove off.

"Who's coming over?" Tyler asked.

"It's a surprise," she replied. She glanced at the review mirror and gave Tyler a warm smile. The drive to their home wouldn't take long.

"Is it someone I know?" he asked.

She shook her head. "Nope."

Her son was inquisitive by nature, and would continue asking her the same question in different ways until he got the answer.

She didn't want to let on to who was stopping by. Otherwise, she wouldn't hear the end of it until Parker arrived.

She'd only been apart from Parker for a short while, and already she was missing him. She couldn't wait to hear his country drawl and feel his strong arms around her again.

"I'm going to cook your favorite dinner tonight," she announced, guiding the car onto their street.

"Lasagna?" he asked hopefully.

"You bet." She giggled, watching him do a little dance in the back seat. "I'm going all out, and we're going to have a nice dinner. Lasagna, garlic bread, and a salad. I'm going to make dessert, too."

"Does this mean I have to take a shower?"

Maddy barked out a laugh at her son. She pulled into their driveway and parked the car. Shutting the engine off, she turned around to face him.

Leave it to her son to try and avoid a bath. He was the typical little boy.

"I'll have to do the smell check to officially make my recommendation."

He burst out cackling. "Momma, you're crazy."

"Crazy for you, baby, and don't you forget it."

———

"Mom, why do I have to clean my room?" Tyler asked, standing in the middle of it with his hands on his hips.

"First of all, because I said so." She leaned against

his doorframe and folded her arms in front of her. His room wasn't the worst it'd ever been, but it could certainly be better. "I want your dirty clothes in the basket, toys organized, then make your bed."

"But our guest won't be coming in my room," he whined, but began doing as she'd instructed while she watched.

"You never know," she responded. She was sure once Tyler met Parker, he would want to show Parker everything.

She grew nervous and glanced at her watch. While Tyler had taken a shower, she had done a once-over on the downstairs rooms.

"So, why is this person coming over?" Tyler closed his closet door. He dropped down on the floor and started arranging his cars and other toys.

"For dinner, and to catch up with each other." She had to think of some excuse that didn't give anything away. She needed to leave before he kept asking questions. "Now hurry up and finish. I'm going to put the lasagna in the oven so it will be hot when our guest arrives."

"Yes, Mom," Tyler mumbled.

She sighed and looked down at her outfit. She had put on a pair of jeans and a comfortable shirt. She was still barefoot, since she hated wearing shoes in the house. She walked downstairs and went into the kitchen.

She'd prepped the lasagna, but held off putting it in the oven. For the special occasion, she'd baked Tyler's favorite peanut butter cookies.

She glanced around at the table she'd set. Three settings instead of two. A silly grin spread across her face. Tonight, they'd share a meal as a family.

She wanted everything to be perfect. This day was long overdue. She could have put her pride aside years ago. She'd known Parker was back home permanently after the injury. News reports on television had talked about the injury, surgeries, and his retirement.

She could have contacted him, but she had chosen to stay away.

Now that was all in the past. Maddy and Parker would start over, at least for Tyler's sake.

One day at a time.

Parker promised he wasn't going anywhere. This was going to be good for Tyler. She'd done the best she could, but her son needed a strong male role model in his life.

She thought about Parker, Wade, and Carson. The Brooks brothers would be the perfect examples for her son. There was no doubt the Brooks brothers would mold her son into the ideal cowboy.

She shuddered at the thought of Jonah.

He hadn't accepted her in the past, but would he accept her son?

Maddy wouldn't stand for anyone being cruel to

him. That was where she drew the line. Jonah may have intimidated her in the past, but she was a grown woman who would protect her child.

Jonah Brooks no longer scared her.

She was back in his son's life, and he was going to have to deal with it.

�   12   ✖

It had taken everything in Parker to hide the rage he'd harbored after finally hearing the truth of what had happened ten years ago. He hadn't wanted to let on to Maddy. He didn't want her to worry about him. So he'd smiled, kissed her, and sent her on her way.

He couldn't go back to the ranch immediately. He needed to calm down first. He'd inherited his temper from his old man, and right now, he was close to exploding. He was strung too damn tight, and wouldn't be responsible for anything he said or did right now.

His father had gone too far. He was not God. He didn't get to decide what happened in people's lives.

Parker tightened his hands on the steering wheel as he drove into town, wanting to find a gift for Tyler. He couldn't show up to the meeting empty-handed.

He was still in shock that he and Maddy had created a life. He didn't know what Tyler looked like, but Parker hoped he had all his momma's qualities. The boy couldn't go wrong with either of his parents' features. According to Maddy and Wade, Tyler wanted to be a cowboy.

Parker grinned and knew which store he would go to. He drove through the town and tried to stay beneath the speed limit. It wouldn't do him any good to get pulled over. It would delay him.

Nothing would keep him from this meeting.

He headed to a store that sold everything a Colorado cowboy would need. He pulled into the parking lot of Smith and Sons, a popular clothing store for the working man.

Parker exited his truck and entered the store. Hopefully, this little expedition would keep his mind off the conversation he was going to have with dear old Dad.

"Can I help you?" a gruff voice asked.

Parker turned to see one of the sales associates from the back.

"Hey, Neil. How are you?" Parker asked.

"Parker, I'm fine. You have to forgive me. From the back, I couldn't tell who you were." Neil laughed as he came forward, his hand out.

Neil had been the manager for years. It was a shop that Parker and his brothers frequented. It wasn't one of the fancy department stores that were in the city, but it was locally owned, and kept up with the latest fashions for men.

Parker chuckled and took his hand in a firm shake. "That's fine. Family good?"

"Yes, everyone is doing well. Kids are growing. Not sure if you've heard, but the missus and I are expecting again." Neil beamed.

"I hadn't heard. Congratulations." Parker slapped him on the back, wanting to share his own news, but it was all too soon. He had to meet his son first. Pride and joy filled Neil's face and had Parker slightly envious. He'd missed that stage of his son's life. He'd been robbed of the excitement of finding out his seed had taken in his woman.

"What are you shopping for today?" Neil asked, breaking him out of his thoughts.

"I'm looking for a special gift. Do you have any new buckles in?" Parker asked.

"We sure do. A truck came this morning, and we just put everything out." Neil waved for him to follow.

They walked over to the wall where the belts were. There was a counter with a glass display case that held all the fancy buckles.

"What type are you looking for? If you can't find what you need, I can grab the catalog from up front and we can order something. Spend fifty bucks, and you get free shipping to your home."

Parker leaned over the glass and carefully assessed

the items in the case. A buckle would complete the cowboy look for Tyler. Maddy had shared with him that Tyler already had a Stetson that he never took off. Parker smiled at the little tidbit of information. They hadn't even met yet, and his boy sounded like him.

"Let me see that one." Parker pointed to a gold-toned buckle that had an image of an eagle on it. That would be perfect for Tyler.

"That is one of the latest ones to come in," Neil said. He took out his keys and unlocked the case. He brought it out and handed it to Parker.

It was a heavy, solid piece. The eagle had its wings spread out wide with a fierce expression on its face.

"It's perfect," Parker muttered.

Their ranch was the Blazing Eagle. Each Brooks man had their family crest tattooed on their right shoulder blade. The eagle meant a lot to their family. It conveyed power, courage, and honesty. Everything he was taught to be from his parents. When his great grandfather had purchased the land, he imagined his family soaring higher than any other, hence why he'd chosen an eagle to represent the Brooks family.

"I'll take it," he announced, looking back to Neil.

No man could call himself a cowboy if he didn't have a decent buckle.

Neil took the buckle. "Great. You said a present. Would you like for me to package it up in a nice gift box?"

They walked toward the front registers.

"Please?" Parker stood by the counter and pulled his wallet out.

"This is a nice piece. Whoever is on the receiving end is a lucky guy." Neil laughed.

Parker thought of Tyler and nodded. "Yes, he is."

———

PARKER DROVE BACK TO THE BLAZING EAGLE RANCH with the radio off. His muscles were tense, unable to relax.

It was time someone put his father in his place.

Parker was going to be that man today. Jonah's meddling had caused Parker to be absent for almost ten years of his son's life. A jolt of pain shot through his chest.

There were some things a boy needed to learn from his father. His boy had missed out on having an influential male figure in his life.

Maddy did the best she could as a single mother, but she shouldn't have had to do it all alone.

Parker couldn't help but think: what if he had never asked to speak with Maddy? Her son—his son—would have grown up not knowing his father was right there in the same town.

He tightened his hands on the steering wheel as he turned down the road that led to the ranch. The steel overhead sign stating The Blazing Eagle Ranch welcomed him.

He scowled.

Parker's entire life, his father had preached about family. The importance of continuing the Brooks name, making sure they all left their legacy for the world to know and love.

Jonah's determination to keep him from Maddy had almost cost him his family.

His breath caught in his throat.

His family.

His throat grew parched at the thought. Maddy and Tyler were his family.

Parker pressed his foot down on the gas. The truck flew forward, eating up the distance. His pickup was able to handle all the dips in the dirt road. The main house was a mile up ahead.

He arrived and parked in front, next to his brothers' trucks. He cut the engine and stormed out the vehicle. He slammed the door shut and stood staring at the home. It had been where he and his brothers were raised.

They'd had a good childhood, without a care in the world. His father pushed his beliefs on the boys, ensuring they would mature into good men. He was stern when it came to discipline, and believed hard work and a rigid work ethic helped grow the man.

Grace Brooks had ensured their house was a home, providing a loving atmosphere where the boys thrived. Grace was the buffer between the boys and their father, the voice of reason in the house. When she spoke, everyone, including Jonah, listened.

While, on the other hand, his son, his flesh and blood, was being raised by a single mother who could barely make ends meet.

Anyway, he came up to her and asked for two boxes of cereal. I could tell she was embarrassed that she had to tell him they could only get one.

The rage that had been harbored inside Parker exploded.

He stalked around the house, searching for his father, ignoring the pain in his knee. His limp was more pronounced, but at the moment, Parker couldn't care less.

He balled his hands into fists, needing to hit something to expel his anger.

Preferably his father.

He rounded on the barn. Carson stepped out and froze in place. His eyes widened with one glance at Parker.

"What the hell is wrong with you?" Carson asked.

"Where is he?" Parker yelled.

Carson tried to grab him, but Parker shook him off. "Who?"

"That son of a bitch father of ours," Parker growled, pushing his Stetson down on his head.

"He's out in the back with Wade viewing the new horses we bought." Carson moved in front of him with his hands raised. "Calm the fuck down. What the hell did he do this time?"

Parker brushed past him, uncaring that his shoulder slammed into his brother's.

"He's gone too far," Parker snapped.

Carson released a curse. Parker could hear his brother following behind him. He cut through the barn to get to the back corral where they let new horses roam free.

He exited the structure. Wade and Jonah stood by the fence deep in conversation. An unfathomable growl escaped Parker as he made his way toward them.

Jonah and Wade turned just as Parker arrived near them.

"You son of a bitch!" Parker hollered. He dove at his father, but two strong arms yanked him back.

"Calm down, Parker," Carson yelled, tightening his hold on Parker.

"What in the hell's got you so wound up, boy?" Jonah snarled. He narrowed his eyes on Parker. "You gonna hit your old man?"

"Let me go." Parker struggled against Carson.

Wade shifted himself between Parker and Jonah.

"What the hell is going on?" Wade asked, his gaze darting from Parker to their father.

"Tell the truth, you lying bastard. This is all your fault!" Parker said through gritted teeth. He dove at their father again, and this time, Wade grabbed Parker's other arm that had broken free from Carson's hold. "She came to the house that day, didn't she?"

Jonah froze in place. He blinked a few times before a sickening smile spread across his face.

"That King gal? That's what this is all about?" Jonah ran a hand along his jaw. He shook his head and wagged a finger at him. "I told you that girl wasn't for you. A Brooks needs to marry someone decent. Someone who's pappy ain't the town drunk."

"Did she come?" Parker screamed. He stopped struggling. He would have been able to break free from his youngest brother, but now that both were holding him back, he wouldn't be able to free himself.

Wade and Carson's grip on him tightened.

Jonah leaned back against the fence. He let loose a chuckle. "I don't understand your infatuation with that gal. You want to know if she came to the house the day you left for Texas? Fine, I'll admit it. Yeah, she did. But I sent her away."

"What?" Parker didn't want to honestly believe his father would be so cruel. Deep in his heart, he believed Maddy. But to hear it come from his father's mouth so nonchalantly, and even seem proud about it, sent Parker into a darker rage.

"Go fuck her a few times so you can get her out of your system. You need to move on to better women," Jonah said matter-of-factly.

"Son of a bitch," Parker snarled.

His brothers had a hard time containing him.

"Calm down, Parker. He's not worth it. Walk away," Wade breathed.

Parker glanced at his brother and saw pity reflecting back at him. He didn't want anyone's pity. He wanted his father to own up and pay for what he had done.

"Are you happy with what you've done?" Parker demanded. He wanted to know how his father truly felt. He thought he knew his father before, but now the blinders were entirely off. "To intervene in my life? To cause me pain like that?"

"Pain? I did you a favor. While you were out on the circuit, don't think I didn't know how you were drinking and whoring around. All the women who threw themselves at you, you wouldn't have thought twice about that King gal. So, you can thank me now." Jonah pushed off the fence and took a step toward him. The older man reached up to his breast pocket and took out a pack of cigarettes. He calmly pulled one out and lit it. He stood staring at Parker while he took a long drag.

"That's enough, Pa," Carson muttered.

"Enough! I'll stop talking when I damn well, please. You boys are going to start listening to me," Jonah snapped, pointing his finger at Parker. "If you don't leave that girl alone, you are out the will. Find yourselves respectable women from good families to settle down with and have child—"

"She was pregnant!" Parker shouted, trying to break free from his brothers. His hat fell to the ground in the scuffle. "She carried my child, and you sent her away. Told her lies about me, and she believed you!"

"What?" Carson shouted.

"Son of a bitch," Wade cursed under his breath.

Parker stood still, his breaths labored. He shook his head, his vision blurring with unshed tears. His emotions were consuming him. First, anger and rage, and now helplessness filled him.

He hadn't been able to be there for Maddy because of the man before him.

"You always preached about family, that we needed to be loyal to each other," Parker spat. How dare his father attempt to instill values into them that he didn't even hold dear to himself. "We are to back each other up, always. We're Brooks. But my son, my flesh and blood, has grown up without his father because of you. My boy...your grandson." Parker's voice cracked. He finally shook his brothers off.

Carson and Wade stood beside him silently. They

both moved closer to Parker. Without saying a word, they had chosen to side with him.

It meant the world to him that his brothers had his back.

That was how Brooks men were to be. Support each other when one was going through a rough patch.

"Pa, how could you?" Wade asked.

Parker pushed a shaky hand through his hair. He didn't care about the tears sliding down his face. How many nights had Maddy cried because she was alone? How many nights was Tyler up sick at night with no one there to help her?

"He doesn't even know me. Where's loyalty in that, Pa?"

Jonah dropped his arm that held the cigarette in it. He glanced away from Parker before turning back to him.

"Damn, Pa. That's fucked up, even for you," Carson said.

The color left Jonah's face, leaving him pale. His eyes grew wide, and his breathing became labored. He took a step toward Parker and wobbled.

"Pa, you okay?" Wade asked. He slowly moved to Jonah.

Jonah grabbed his chest as his knees buckled. He collapsed to the ground.

His brothers rushed over to Jonah. Parker fell to his

knees, tears streaming down his face. There was no more fight left in him.

Time appeared to pass in slow motion.

Carson shook their father while screaming his name.

Wade snatched his phone from his back pocket and made a call.

Parker sat rooted in place, his gaze locked with his father's glassy eyes.

13

"Mom, I'm starving," Tyler whined. He came and plopped down on the couch next to Maddy.

She sighed and turned to him with a faint smile.

"What time is the person getting here?"

"Our guest is a real person. I'm sure something just held them up."

Tyler slouched down in his seat. His hat shifted over his eyes. "But you said they would be here by six, and it's after six now."

She glanced over at her cell and saw that Tyler was indeed correct. It was a quarter after six, and still no word from Parker. She chewed on her lip with worry.

"I'm sure something came up and he's just running late. He really wanted to come to meet you."

Tyler pushed his hat up and looked at her suspiciously. "Why would he want to come meet me?"

Her son was just too smart and inquisitive.

When he'd come down from cleaning his room, she had sent him right back upstairs to shower. She didn't know what had transpired in his room from the time she'd left to when he'd finished, but he was a little musty and disheveled.

While he was in the shower, she'd gone through his closet and pulled out his best jeans, ones without holes in them, and a nice clean shirt. His ever-faithful cowboy hat rounded out the outfit.

One day, he would have to part with that darn hat when the seams came undone or he outgrew it. When that day came, she knew she might as well give in and just buy him a new one.

"Because he heard how awesome of a kid you are." She playfully reached out and tickled his stomach.

He laughed and rolled away from her to the edge of the couch. Tyler was extremely ticklish, and Maddy had always taken advantage of it since he was a little boy.

"Can I watch television?"

"Sure." She tossed him the remote.

He took it and flipped through the channels until he found a popular cartoon show he liked to watch.

Another fifteen minutes went by, and now Maddy was panicking.

Had Parker changed his mind?

Was this all too soon?

Maybe she shouldn't have told him about Tyler yet. When she'd been at the creek with him, her gut had told her to go ahead and tell him everything. There was no way she'd be able to live in a town and raise his child without him knowing. It had to be done.

"Mom, my stomach is growling. I could eat a bear right now," Tyler groaned. He had transitioned to the floor in front of the television.

She just prayed stains didn't magically appear on his fresh clothes. It would seem her son was a dirt magnet.

"I'd like to see you try." She snorted. "You'd have to fight and kill it first. Then who'd skin it?"

"Mom, that's gross."

She shrugged. "You said you could eat a bear."

"It was a figure of speech, Mom. I wouldn't really eat a bear." Tyler dramatically rolled his eyes.

Maddy glanced into the kitchen. Dinner was ready and the table was set.

The only person missing was Parker.

She looked around their sparse little house. She'd decorated as best as she could to make it feel like a home. She'd had a blast shopping around at the second-hand stores. There were some great finds that didn't cost her an arm and a leg. She was proud of the home she'd created for her and Tyler. They had everything they needed.

Maddy picked up her cell phone again to make sure she hadn't missed a call, but nothing.

"I'll be back, buddy," she said, but Tyler was engrossed in his show once again. She stood and walked into the kitchen. There were no text messages from Parker. She was two seconds away from panicking now.

Should she call him?

She blew out a deep breath and remembered the last time she hadn't taken the initiative.

It got her to be a single mother to a beautiful little boy.

Mind made up, she scrolled through her contacts and found Parker's name.

She placed the phone to her ear and listened to it ring.

Her heart was pounding as it rang again.

"Maddy girl. I'm so sorry. I was just about to call you," Parker's deep drawl came through the line.

Her heart sank.

He wasn't coming.

She braced herself for whatever reason he was about to give her. All the doubts she had had come full circle on her.

"What's going on? Is everything all right?" she asked. She tried to play it cool and not reveal her true feelings. It was unlike Parker to not show when he said he would. One thing she was sure of about him was that he was a man of his word.

She moved to the doorframe where she could peek in on Tyler. He was in the exact same spot he was in when she'd stepped from the room. His hat was placed on the floor beside him, and she could tell he'd run his hands through his dark curls, leaving them going every which way.

"No," Parker breathed.

She froze in place and bit her lip. Her eyes fluttered closed as she waited.

"My father had a heart attack. We're at the hospital now. They rushed him into surgery to work on him," Parker continued.

"Oh my goodness!" she cried out. That hadn't been what she had expected Parker to say. She didn't like Jonah, and thought he was an evil man, but never would she wish something like this on him.

She wouldn't wish anything bad on anyone.

"My brothers and I are waiting to hear something. I can't leave now."

"I completely understand. Parker, I'm so sorry to hear this," she stated. She leaned back against the doorframe. The need to go to him was strong, but she didn't want to intrude on this tense time for his family. "We can do this another night."

"No," Parker said. "It's been way too long already. I want to meet him. Tonight. Can you bring him here?" Parker asked.

She hesitated. Did she want to drag her son out to the hospital?

Parker must have picked up on her brief pause. "He can meet Carson and see Wade again. I need him here, Maddy girl."

She closed her eyes and nodded, even though he couldn't see her. "Of course. We'll be on our way."

"Thanks, Maddy. It means more to me than you know."

———

MADDY EYED THE ENTRANCE OF GENERAL HOSPITAL. It was located one town over from Shady Springs. She shuddered, remembering the last time she'd had to come here.

It was the night her mother had gotten the call that her father had been rushed to the hospital.

He'd never made it. By the time he was found in the alley and the ambulance was called, he was pronounced dead on arrival. She and her mother had reached the hospital in time to identify the body.

"Mom, is your friend okay?" Tyler asked from the back seat. She had packed him a few snacks to tide him over until she could get them real food. Of course, being as hungry as he was, he'd eaten almost everything within minutes of being in the car.

She blinked and turned to look at him. "Yeah, but his father isn't. We're going to go up to see him for support. This is a hard time for the family, and they need us."

Tyler nodded, apparently understanding the grave nature of the visit. "Okay."

"Come on, big guy." She grabbed her purse and exited the car.

She watched as Tyler stepped from the vehicle and shut his door. He walked around the car and took her hand.

They wandered inside the glass sliding doors and over to the information desk.

The woman behind the desk glanced up from her computer. "Hello, can I help you?"

"Hi. I'm looking for the family of Jonah Brooks." Maddy stood tall. Never would she have thought she'd be at the hospital for Jonah.

She pushed her pettiness aside and remembered she wasn't at the hospital for him.

She was there for Parker, Wade, and Carson.

The woman typed out a few commands on her keyboard before turning back to Maddy. "Second floor. The intensive care unit will be at the end of the hallway, but the family waiting room is next to the entrance to the ICU. You'll see a frosted glass door and windows. That should be where they are. It would seem the patient is still in surgery."

Maddy swallowed hard and jerked her head in a nod.

"Thanks."

She held on to Tyler's hand, not wanting to let go. She needed to feel his little hand in hers as they made their way to the elevator. They quietly waited for the doors to open. Once the elevator arrived, they stepped on. Maddy pushed the button for the second floor and blew out a deep breath.

"It's going to be okay, Mom," Tyler said.

Maddy glanced at him in shock. His keen eyes watched her. She offered him a small smile. "I know, baby. Hospitals give me the heebie-jeebies."

The doors opened with a feminine computerized voice announcing the floor.

"Can you tell me who we're meeting now?" he asked, walking alongside her.

"Be patient," she said in a singsong voice. She looked around and saw the landmarks the woman at the information desk had given her. "Come on. This way."

Her gaze landed on the frosted glass door and window. A sign plate was on the wall that read: Family Waiting Room.

Her heart slammed into her chest. She swallowed hard as they got closer to the waiting room.

"Mom, you're squeezing my hand hard," Tyler complained.

"I'm sorry," she whispered. She loosened her grip on Tyler and rubbed it with her other hand.

They stopped in front of the door. She eyed Tyler,

who was staring off down the hospital hallway that led to another nursing unit.

Now or never, Maddy, she thought to herself.

She gripped the door handle and pulled it open. They stepped inside the room and paused.

Parker sat in a chair across the small room with his elbows braced on his knees. He held his head in his hands, unaware she was there. Wade and Carson sat on opposite sides of the room.

The door shut, and all eyes landed on her and Tyler.

Tyler took a step closer to Maddy.

She glanced down at him. "It's okay, buddy," she whispered.

He tightened his grip on her hand.

Parker stood from his seat and cleared his throat. His gaze was locked on Tyler.

Her attention moved from Parker to Tyler and back, and it hit her how strong the resemblance was between them.

How had she not seen it before?

Tyler had Parker's mannerisms, the love of a dusty old hat, and the same striking eyes. Everything about her son screamed Parker. The only thing he got from her was his darker hair color and a permanent tan.

"Mom, that's the cowboy from the store," Tyler whispered, yanking on her hand.

Wade chuckled and stood from his seat. "How are you, Tyler?" he asked.

Carson stood up with awe in his eyes.

Parker had yet to take his eyes off of Tyler.

"I'm okay, Mr. Brooks." Tyler leaned against her.

She was shocked at his shy demeanor. Tyler King was never shy around new people, and she didn't know where this behavior was coming from.

"Can I still come to the camp with the horses?"

Wade chuckled. "Your mother and I will talk about it today, buddy. Is that okay?"

Tyler jerked his head in a nod. Leave it up to him to still be thinking of the camp and horses.

Maddy guided Tyler to stand in front of her. He was almost her height, so she stepped slightly to the side and rested her hands on his shoulders.

"Tyler, I'd like to officially introduce you to your Uncle Wade."

Wade tipped his head to Tyler with a wide grin on his lips.

She pointed to Carson. "This is your Uncle Carson. He loves football just like you do."

Tyler glanced at her with wide eyes.

"It's nice to finally meet you, Tyler," Carson said. He flipped his baseball cap around so the brim was in the back.

"Nice to meet you, too," Tyler said.

"What's your favorite position?" Carson asked, folding his arms in front of his chest.

"Quarterback," Tyler immediately responded.

Maddy knew the basics of football. From his previous coaches, they'd all gushed about her son's throwing arm.

"Is that so? I was a quarterback all throughout high school and college." Carson's face lit up. "We're going to have to throw the old pigskin around when we get a chance."

Tyler nodded. "Anytime. I mean, as long as my momma is okay with it."

Maddy squeezed his shoulders. Her throat tightened with the last introduction that needed to be made.

"And, Tyler..." Her voice cracked. She wrapped her arms around his chest and brought him back to her for a hug. "This is Parker, your father."

Tyler stilled under her hold and turned to face her. For the first time, he appeared to be rendered speechless.

"You mean it, Mom?"

She nodded.

He glanced back at Parker and leaned into her. "He's a cowboy like you said," he whispered loudly.

A laugh escaped her. Her vision blurred with tears. Tyler twisted around.

Parker cleared his throat. He appeared nervous and uncertain. "Hey, Tyler. I've been waiting a long time to meet you, buddy. I have a gift for you."

Maddy's eyebrows rose sharply. "It's okay, buddy."

She pushed Tyler forward, who cautiously walked

over to the three towering men. He looked each of the Brooks brothers up and down before settling his sights on Parker. He stared up at his father as if memorizing his features. If only she knew what her son was thinking. He'd been waiting for this day for a long time.

She'd hated when activities at school called for the men in the family to step up and come. Tyler hadn't had that. It had just been her and him. Some of his friends' fathers had taken Tyler under their wings so he wouldn't be left out. She blinked back tears.

The look of awe plastered on the Brooks brothers' faces was heartwarming. If the new school had 'Donuts with Dad' like his previous school, he now had his father, and she was pretty confident two uncles who would be showing up.

Parker picked up a small box that sat on the chair beside his. It had a bow wrapped around it, and he handed it to Tyler.

"Thank you," Tyler said. He glanced back at Maddy first before rotating back to Parker. "But I don't have a gift for you."

Wade and Carson chuckled.

Parker's featured relaxed as a grin spread across his face. He pointed to the box. "That's okay, buddy. Believe me, you've given me the best gift anyone could ever give."

She bit her lip to keep from crying. She dug around

in her purse, looking for tissues. Of course, she had none.

"I hear you wanted to be a cowboy someday and figured you might need this," Parker said.

Tyler worked on opening the box. The ribbon fell to the floor, ignored. Tyler finally got it open, and his sharp intake of breath had Maddy curious.

What the heck could Parker have gone and bought that quick?

"Wow! This is so cool!" Tyler shouted. He flew around to face her. "Momma, look! A real cowboy belt buckle."

He held it up, and the damn thing was almost the size of the state of Colorado. Her son was tall for his age, but skinny. She would be surprised if he would be able to walk with it on.

Tyler spun around and flew forward, wrapping his arms around Parker's waist.

The tears fell from her eyelids as she watched her son with his father.

This was long overdue.

14

Parker froze at first, but then his natural instincts kicked in. Tyler's arms were squeezing him tight. Parker folded his arms around his son and held on to him as if his life depended on it. He'd only known about his son for a day, but it felt as if he'd missed him for an eternity.

His son.

In the flesh.

Immediately, he was in love with the little boy who was his mirror image, with some of his momma thrown in.

Tyler's face lighting up at the sight of the buckle let him know it was the perfect gift. Just to see that face again, Parker would do anything.

"I knew you would come for us." Tyler's voice was

muffled by Parker's shirt. Tyler tightened his hold on Parker.

His gut clenched at Tyler's innocence. His son had faith that one day he would come. Parker vowed that moment, he'd do whatever he must to not let his son down.

"Momma said one day we'd meet."

"I'm not ever going away from you again, Tyler." Parker's voice grew gruff with emotion.

Tyler tipped his head back and looked up at him. His breath was snatched from his chest as he stared down at the same steel-gray eyes that were identical to Parker and his brothers. He knew without a doubt, this boy was his. He may not have his last name, but he had Brooks blood running through his veins.

"None of us are going anywhere, little guy," Carson said, stepping forward to squeeze Tyler's shoulders.

Parker glanced at his brothers and found their faces wet with tears. Carson wiped his face with the back of his shirt sleeve.

"Sure aren't." Wade sniffed. He used the back of his hand to dry his cheeks. He stepped forward and clapped Tyler on the back. "We're going to bring you out to the farm. You can ride all the horses you want and learn how to become a cowboy."

Parker glanced up and found Maddy standing across the room with tears streaming down her face.

"Come here, Maddy girl." He opened his other arm out to her. At the moment, he refused to let Tyler go, and seeing how he was gripping his shirt, he didn't want to let Parker go either.

Maddy flew across the room and into his arms. Parker brought both of them flush against him.

He had a family.

Parker caught sight of Wade and Carson, rubbing their faces again.

"I'm going to make this right, I promise," Parker murmured, his lips brushing across Maddy's forehead.

Parker felt complete and whole with Maddy and Tyler in his arms.

"Hey, we're going to run down to the cafeteria to grab some coffee. Anyone want anything?" Wade asked.

"I'll take a coffee," Parker replied.

Maddy curved around, but kept one arm around Parker. "Me, too."

"Can we get you anything, little man?" Carson asked Tyler.

His son mimicked his mother and nodded. "Can I get a juice and something to eat? I'm hungry enough to eat a bear—I mean, um..."

"Me, too." Carson patted his flat abdomen. "I could eat a bear. Could probably fight one now, too, just to get food."

Tyler's eyes widened, and he shot a glance at his

mother, who burst out laughing. Tyler giggled at whatever their shared look meant. Parker wasn't sure what was going on, but he was glad to see them smiling.

"We'll grab sandwiches or whatever they've got down there and bring it up," Wade announced.

"Thanks." Parker nodded to his brothers.

They turned and stepped out of the room quietly. He knew without them saying it, but they were trying to give him some time with Maddy and Tyler alone.

"Here, let's have a seat." Maddy waved a hand to the chairs behind them.

Parker sat with Maddy and Tyler on either side of him. Tyler was practically glued to his hip, and at the moment, he wouldn't have it any other way. "Let me put the buckle back in the box so you don't drop it."

Tyler handed it to her. She snagged the box from the floor and tucked it back inside before placing the box on the table next to her.

"What was that look and laugh about?" he asked, curious as to what had passed between them.

Tyler glanced at his mother, then turned to him. "Earlier, I told Mom that I was hungry enough to eat a bear. She told me that she'd liked to see me catch a bear, kill the bear, and then skin it so I could eat it."

"I sure did." Maddy gave an unladylike snort.

Parker chuckled. "Well, a bear would be a tough catch."

"But Uncle Carson said he could probably fight a bear. Has he ever gone up against one?" Tyler asked.

"No, but we've scared them off from the ranch plenty of times. That's one thing about living in Colorado in the country. The open land is home to all kinds of wildlife."

"Wow." Tyler sighed.

The room grew quiet. Parker couldn't even begin to describe what he was feeling at the moment. He was just happy he had Maddy and Tyler with him.

"Looks like we have plenty of time to kill now," Parker began. He had so many questions for Tyler, and he was sure Tyler had some for him, too. Since they still hadn't heard any word from the doctors since they'd first taken Jonah back to surgery, they might as well start getting to know one another. "Why don't we ask each other questions."

"Okay. That would be cool." Tyler nodded. His brow furrowed for a second, as if thinking of the perfect questions. "Do you have a horse?"

Parker laughed. He rested his arm on the back of Tyler's chair. He pushed his hat back slightly so he could see Tyler.

"Of course I do. His name is Bandit."

"Wow. That's a cool name." Tyler's eyes grew wide. "One day I'm going to get a horse, and I need a cool name like that."

Parker mentally ran through the mares they had at

the ranch. He hadn't had a chance to check out the new ones yet, but if none fit Tyler, then Parker would go out and find the boy one. A cowboy always had a trusty steed he could call his own.

"I'd say wait until you get one. You have to learn his ways and personality. That will help the name come."

Parker sensed Maddy's gaze on him. She was still close enough where he could feel her hip brush against his. She chuckled at the next question.

"Have you ever been thrown off a horse?"

"Hell—I mean, heck yeah. Plenty of times, too." Parker snickered, thinking of all the times he'd been thrown as a kid. He'd broken plenty of bones, and sported tons of bruises growing up. "Now, when I used to get thrown off the bulls, that was something else."

Tyler froze. His mouth opened and shut as if he were in shock. Maddy slapped a hand over her mouth to muffle her laugh that morphed into a cough.

"Bulls?" Tyler slowly repeated. He appeared like he had to process what Parker was saying.

"I was a bull rider when I met your mother." Parker glanced at her. "That's what I was doing when you were born."

Maddy's smile disappeared. They stared at each other, Parker lost in his own world, remembering leaving town after she'd gone.

"Oh my goodness!" Tyler screeched. He jumped up from the chair and turned to Maddy with excitement lining his face. "Mom, I have to call Chad and Jason and tell them about Parker. They are not going to believe he was a bull rider."

"Tomorrow, young man. It's way too late for you to be calling anyone," Maddy said, peering at her watch.

Tyler flopped back down in his chair, rattling questions off. Parker tried to keep up with them. He even threw in some questions of his own.

Parker couldn't stop staring at Tyler. It was like seeing his younger clone. Where Parker had a deep tan from being out in the sun for countless hours, Tyler's skin tone was more profound than his. He was a pure mixture of Parker and Maddy.

"Let me see you," Parker said. He removed Tyler's hat from his head. His hair was dark brown and curly, just like his was.

Tyler reached up and removed his hat as if he, too, wanted to study Parker. They stared at each other before falling into a fit of laughter.

———

Carson and Wade had returned from their trip with food and drinks.

Tyler had moved over and was talking with Wade and Carson. Or, better yet, throwing random questions at them. Laughter filled the air as they answered each and every one.

Parker peeked over at Maddy, who was quietly sipping on her coffee. She glanced at him and offered a small smile.

"You okay?" she asked. She leaned close to Parker and bumped him gently with her shoulder.

"Yeah, as good as I can expect right now." He lifted his cup and took a swig of the strong coffee from the cafeteria. He didn't know what they did to it, but he was confident he was going to be wired for the rest of the night.

Having Maddy and Tyler there helped break up the tension while they waited for the doctors to come in and update them.

Parker sat back in his chair and breathed in deeply. He didn't want to believe that the events on the ranch caused his father's heart issues.

Jonah Brooks was as healthy as a horse. The man had smoked like a freight train for as long as Parker could remember, and was never really sick. In Parker's eyes, his mule-headed father was invincible.

He replayed everything that had occurred at the ranch, and he couldn't say he would do anything different. He couldn't help going off on his father.

Hell, what man wouldn't after finding out his father had a hand in almost ruining not one person's life, but three?

What his father had done was unforgivable.

How could Jonah be so narrow-minded to not see Parker and Maddy were right for each other?

She wasn't her father.

She was a decent, honest woman who worked hard since she was fifteen years old. But Jonah wouldn't have known that. He only knew who her father was, and that was all he cared to know.

The room fell into a comfortable silence.

"Who are we waiting for again?" Tyler asked Maddy. "Who's sick?"

Maddy glanced his way. He motioned for Tyler to come and sit next to him.

"My father, your Papa Jonah, got really sick out at the ranch today," Parker began gently. He left out the minute details of the argument and fighting that had been going on. "He had a heart problem that no one knew about, and the doctors are trying to fix him now."

"Will he be okay?" Tyler asked.

Parker rubbed his back. "I hope so, buddy."

Parker leaned back and rested his head on the wall behind him. No matter how upset he was at his father, he would never wish death on him.

How the hell had Jonah Brooks had a heart attack?

Parker would have believed pigs were flying before he'd think his father had heart issues. He was the toughest son of a bitch Parker knew. If anything was going to take his father out, Parker would have put his money on lung cancer.

If Jonah pulled through, maybe they could continue their conversation in a more civilized manner.

The door to the room opened, and a team of doctors entered. Parker immediately tensed. Dread filled his stomach as the newcomers filed in.

"Brooks family?" A physician in blue scrubs and a surgical cap stepped forward.

Parker, Wade, and Carson stood. Maddy moved over and sat with Tyler.

Parker moved toward the group and spoke first. "I'm Parker Brooks. These are my brothers, Wade and Carson.

"Hello, I'm Dr. Mizen." He shook all three of the brothers' hands.

Parker didn't like the grave expression on the man's face. Parker glanced at the other people who stood behind the doctor. Some appeared barely legal enough to buy alcohol, while others looked around his age. His heart raced at the unknown of what they were about to be told.

"I'm the surgeon who led the team on your father's surgery."

"Hope you have good news for us, Doc," Wade muttered.

"The surgery went well. We found a few severe blockages in the major arteries that surround your father's heart. They were all totally occluded, meaning there was a lack of blood supplying the heart muscle."

Parker shared a concerned glance with his brothers.

"Is he going to make it?" Carson asked.

Parker folded his arms in front of his chest, unable to believe what he was hearing.

"We were able to do bypasses and reroute blood flow to help feed the heart muscle. Now, Mr. Brooks did suffer some damage to his heart muscle, and it is weakened. Once he wakes up, there will be a long road to recovery, but I think overall, he should do fine."

Parker blew out a deep breath. He took his hat off and ran a trembling hand through his hair.

"When can we see him?" Wade asked.

"He's in the recovery area now, and should be moved to intensive care soon." The doctor's face relaxed slightly. "It's a good thing y'all called the ambulance when you did, or he wouldn't have made it. He suffered what is commonly known as the 'widow maker.'"

Parker didn't need a fancy medical degree to understand the term.

"Thank you, Doc," Parker said, clearing his throat. He reached out and shook the doctor's hand again, as did Wade and Carson. "We appreciate all you and your team have done."

"It shouldn't be too much longer. Once Mr. Brooks is settled, I'll make sure the nurses grab you so you can see him. It can't be for long, though. Visiting hours for the intensive care unit are about over, but we'll make an exception since he just got out of surgery."

"Thanks again, Doc," Wade said.

The team exited the room.

Dr. Mizen paused at the door and glanced back at them. "Hang in there, family. He's not out of the woods quite yet. Goodnight." He gave another nod and shut the door behind him.

They all settled back down and waited. An hour later, a tiny young woman dressed in pink scrubs appeared at the door.

Tyler was tucked under his arm and dozing off. Maddy, on his other side, played a game on her cellphone. They'd all gone through plenty of coffee, but they all looked drained. Parker felt as if he'd been on a cattle drive for weeks he was so tired.

"Brooks family?" she asked. Her gaze flickered between them.

"Yeah, that us," Carson muttered. He scrubbed a hand over his face and stood from his chair.

"Okay. You all can come back to see Mr. Brooks, but it would have to be one at a time because the area is tight."

Parker glanced at Carson and Wade. "Y'all can go first."

Carson disappeared from the room with the nurse.

Wade turned to Parker. "Is it me, or does this feel like a dream?"

"I never thought I'd see the old man in the hospital like this." Parker shook his head, tightening his grip on

Tyler. He removed the boy's hat and placed it on an empty chair near them. He pressed a kiss to his son's head.

"He was always bigger than life. I thought the ornery son of a bitch would outlive us." Wade blew out a deep breath.

"He still may," Parker muttered.

Minutes later, Carson returned. He looked haggard and weary. He plopped down in his chair and leaned his head back against the wall. He stared up at the ceiling, lost in thought.

Parker let him be. This was all hitting them hard.

Wade left next with the nurse.

The room remained silent. It was close to two in the morning, and it was a wonder they all hadn't passed out in the waiting room.

Minutes later, Wade came back. He jerked his head to Parker. The nurse waited at the door patiently with a small smile.

Parker glanced at Maddy, unsure if he wanted to see his father.

"Go," she whispered. She leaned up and placed a kiss on his cheek. She patted his thigh and offered him a tired smile. "We'll be here waiting for you."

He nodded. He stood carefully and held Tyler up so she could slide in to take his place. She tucked a sleeping Tyler under her arm and held him close.

Parker turned and followed the nurse out of the

room. She led him to through a set of double doors next to the waiting room. The nursing area was bustling with people going in and out of the small individual rooms. Finally, she stopped at a secluded one in the corner.

She had been right.

There wasn't much room for one person with all the machines surrounding his father's bed.

There were so many lines coming and going from around Jonah. There was a plastic apparatus exiting from his mouth. It was connected to a machine beside the bed that appeared to be helping him breathe.

"I'll be outside the door if you need anything. Just a few minutes, please," the nurse whispered.

Parker jerked his head in a nod, unable to take his eyes off his father. He stood at the foot of the bed and rested his hands on the foot rail.

"I don't know if you can hear me, Pa," he began. He blew out a shaky breath, unsure of what to say exactly. "When you get better and are released from here, we are going to have a long talk, man to man. Civilized this time. Maddy is back in my life, and now it's for good. I don't need your blessing, because she's the one for me."

He paused, trying to contain his emotions. Growing up, Jonah wasn't a man who shared his feelings or emotions with the boys.

"That was women's stuff," Jonah had said in his gruff manner.

Grace, on the other hand, always wanted the boys to talk out their problems.

"And Tyler, your grandson, he's amazing, Pa." Parker cleared his throat. "He's just like me. He's a true Brooks, and we always take care of our own. It's not time for you to join Momma yet. Pull through this, Pa. Fight."

Parker turned and left the room.

He'd said all he needed to say.

15

Maddy leaned back and closed her eyes. Parker had insisted on driving her and Tyler home. They had left Maddy's car in the hospital parking lot. His brothers would make sure her car got home later. She was drained from sitting in that waiting room for so long.

Soft country music played while they rode in silence. Tyler was fast asleep in the back seat. It was a good thing that Parker drove them. There was no way she'd be able to carry Tyler from the car, much less inside and upstairs. He was almost the same size she was.

She sensed the truck slowing down. Her eyes opened, and she recognized the street. They were almost to their house.

"It's the one with the porch light on." She pointed

to her home. It was late, and when she'd left, she figured they would be returning after dark.

Parker nodded. He guided the vehicle into her driveway and parked. He turned to her and took her hand in his. He brought it up to his lips and placed a kiss to the back of her hand.

"Thanks for coming," he murmured.

"Of course," she whispered.

He entwined their fingers and stared down at their hands.

"Are you going to tell me about what happened at the ranch earlier?" she asked.

She'd sensed some guilt in Parker at the hospital. None of them spoke a word of what had happened before Jonah was rushed to the hospital. But if she knew Parker like she thought she did, she was sure something had gone down on the ranch.

He shook his head. "Not tonight."

He brought his eyes back up, and she saw the pain in them.

"Okay. If you want to talk, I'm here," she whispered. She may not be able to help with the relationship between him and his father, but at least she could be a shoulder he could lean on, and offer an ear for him to get some things off his chest.

He pressed another kiss to her hand and released it. He stepped from the vehicle. She watched him walk around the truck to her door. He opened it and helped her down before moving to Tyler's.

Maddy dug around in her purse to find her keys. She took them out just as Parker pulled Tyler out. He lifted him up and carried him to the porch behind Maddy.

They entered the house, and she showed him to Tyler's room. Together, they undressed the sleeping angel and tucked him into his bed. Parker draped the covers up over their son. He ran a hand over Tyler's head and pressed a kiss to this forehead.

Maddy was an emotional wreck.

Parker had been so kind and patient with Tyler in the short time they'd had getting to know each other. She had to pinch herself to make sure she wasn't dreaming.

Parker followed Maddy from the room. She quietly shut the door. She leaned against the wall and stared at Parker. He appeared drained. He took his hat off and slid a hand through his hair. His curls were a tangled mess from the hat and him running his hands through it all day.

He glanced up at her, and her breath caught in her throat.

Even though he seemed dead on his feet, he was the sexist man she'd ever seen.

"Thanks again, Maddy girl." His voice was low and gruff.

It sent chills down her spine.

"It's late, and you shouldn't have to drive home at this hour. Why don't you stay the night?" she asked. She clasped her hands together in front of her. She tried to keep all emotions from her face, but she was sure she failed.

Parker stepped forward, trapping her against the wall with his body. He reached up and ran a single finger down the side of her face.

"Maddy girl," he breathed.

"You look exhausted, and I just want to lie with you," she murmured, playing with a button on his shirt.

"If I stay, there'd be more." He chuckled.

She smiled, and felt her sassy nature come out. "I wouldn't expect anything less."

She leaned up and kissed his chin. She took his hand and led him to her bedroom.

Parker tossed his hat on the chair in the corner and sat on the bed to remove his boots.

Maddy rushed into the bathroom and shut the door. She quickly relieved her bladder. She washed her hands, then proceeded to brush her teeth. This was the first time in years she'd had a man spend the night with her. She dragged her brush through her hair to untangle it before wrapping it up with her silk scarf.

She stared at herself in the mirror and breathed in deeply.

Parker was in her home.

She closed her eyes and sent up a prayer that this wasn't a dream, and everything would work out as he'd promised.

Maddy exited the room to find Parker sitting on the edge of her bed with just his jeans on. His perfectly sculpted chest was on display.

"All yours," she said. She cleared her throat, not knowing why her voice went husky.

Parker nodded and headed into the bathroom. She dashed into her closet to find something to sleep in. She changed into a soft, cotton nightie. It wasn't sexy by any means, but it was cute and feminine. It had spaghetti straps and stopped mid-thigh.

She walked out of her closet just in time to catch sight of a very naked Parker climbing into her bed. Her knees grew weak as she walked to the other side of the bed. She climbed in and shut the light off on her nightstand.

Parker immediately pulled her to him and tucked her into the crook of his arm.

"Just let me get in a short nap, then I'll be ready for ya, darlin'," he drawled.

Maddy patted him on his chest and rolled her eyes. His eyes were already drooping shut.

"Sure, big guy," she said softly. She was content with them lying together in the bed.

"I'm serious. We have a lot of making up to do." He yawned.

She didn't believe a word he said. She smiled and nestled into him. His hard body pressed up against her softer one had her feeling secure. She leaned her head back to study him.

A soft snore escaped him.

Sleep.

She didn't know what the future held, but she was willing to take it one step at a time to figure it out.

At the moment, she felt safe in his arms, and trusted he meant every word he'd said.

She closed her eyes and allowed herself to drift off into a peaceful sleep.

MADDY TURNED HER HEAD ON HER PILLOW, AND A shiver took over her body. She smiled, loving her dream. She sighed, enjoying the pleasure that rocked through her.

She paused.

How could a dream be so real?

What the hell? Might as well enjoy the realistic dream. She settled back and shifted in the bed. Her mystery lover pressed featherlight kisses along her stomach.

She'd had sex dreams before, but never something as realistic as this.

Warm hands spread her legs apart.

A moan slipped from her.

Her body was burning with a need that she'd never felt before in…a dream…

Wait a minute.

Her clit was swollen and being gently tugged.

Her eyes flew open.

This was no dream.

Her gaze dropped down and found Parker's head between her thighs.

His eyes flickered up to hers. "It's about time you joined this little party, Maddy girl," he drawled.

His tongue slid between her folds.

Maddy couldn't hold back the groan that slipped from her lips.

"Parker," she gasped.

He latched on to her clit, taking her breath away.

Her back arched off the bed. She became tangled in her nightie as it twisted around her chest. She didn't know how the hell it had gotten to where it was, but it had to go.

Maddy wrestled the material up and over her head. She tossed it to the floor.

Parker took his time working her body. She writhed, unable to control herself. She didn't know how long she'd been asleep, but that much time couldn't have passed.

She shouldn't have underestimated Parker. Apparently, when he put his mind to something, it was just as good as done.

She threaded her fingers into his thick hair. She needed to have something to hold on to for this ride.

He pushed two fingers inside her. She cried out from the invasion. His tongue flicked along her clit, teasing her.

Making her cry out in pleasure.

"You might want to keep it down." Parker chuckled. He lifted his head and met her gaze.

She released a curse. Why the hell didn't she think about that? Tyler was asleep in the bedroom next to hers.

"I'm sorry," she moaned.

He continued to slowly thrust his fingers in and out of her.

"Hell, I'd love to hear you come on my tongue, but I doubt we want to explain to our son why his momma was screaming my name." His eyes crinkled in the corners while his lips tilted up in that dangerous grin of his.

Her body trembled from the sensations coursing through her.

"I'm not going to scream," she whispered.

He cocked an eyebrow at her. His hand paused, his fingers still lodged deep inside her.

"Oh, really?" A devilish glint appeared in his eyes.

Oh shit.

She'd just unknowingly issued a challenge.

Parker was competitive by nature. Hell, the man rode bulls for a living. He was one of three boys who all participated in some type of sport.

What the hell had she just done?

Well, she was going to have to pull up her big girl panties and make this challenge official.

"Yeah, really," she murmured. She rotated her hips, not breaking their gaze. Her breath caught in her throat at the darkening of his gray eyes. "I'm not going to scream."

"Is that so?" He drew his hand back and rotated his fingers ever so slightly before slowly pushing them deep.

"Fuck," she breathed.

A shudder passed through her. He was deliberately torturing her, and the man had the nerve to smile while he did it. Her eyes fluttered closed for a brief second before opening.

"Hmmm..." he murmured. He nipped her inner thigh, and she jumped. "I make you scream with my tongue, you're answering Tyler's questions."

"Okay. But if I don't?"

Parker's lips spread into his heart-stopping grin. "Then you'll be screaming on my cock."

He leaned down and captured her clit with his lips, and she was a goner.

She should have known not to play with fire, and right now, her body was going up in flames.

Parker didn't hold anything back.

He gave her his all.

She tried her best to remain silent. They were playing a dangerous game. Tyler could wake up at any moment and come knock on her door.

Something about the chance of getting caught again heightened her arousal. It was as if they were two teenagers trying to sneak to have fun and not be discovered by their parents.

"Parker," she moaned. She pulled on his hair, and her hips thrust against him, trying to reach that magical place that was just out of her reach.

"Come on, Maddy girl. Let. Go."

He pulled her clit into his mouth with hard sucking motions, while his fingers twisted around and hit her sweet spot.

Maddy's body detonated.

She snatched a pillow from the bed and held it over her face just as her cry of pleasure erupted from her lips.

Her body trembled with the force of her orgasm.

She held on to the pillow with a death grip, unable to believe how hard her release was. Her body finally relaxed back on the bed, but she kept her face covered.

"Maddy girl." Parker chuckled.

Her cheeks burned from embarrassment. She just prayed the pillow did its job to muffle her. There was no way she would be having the full-on birds and bees talk with Tyler at this age.

Parker tugged on the pillow, but she refused to let it go.

"What are you hiding behind the pillow for?" He jerked harder, ripping it out of her grasp. "Are you ashamed of the way your body reacted to me?" he asked. His eyebrows rose high.

"No," she responded softly.

He pushed up off the bed and climbed over her. He rested his hands on both sides of her head. A feral glint appeared in his eyes. She swallowed hard. Her gaze slid along his chest and down to his thick length brushing up against her core. "I want you inside me."

She reached up and tugged his head down. His lips molded to hers in a deep, passionate kiss. Parker immediately dominated it. He rested himself in the valley of her thighs. Her breasts were crushed between them. She wrapped her arms around his neck while returning his kiss with the same fierceness.

Parker tore his mouth from hers. He lifted himself briefly and guided the blunt tip of his cock to her slick opening.

Their eyes met as he slowly sank inside her.

"Fuck," Parker groaned. "Maddy girl, you feel so fucking good."

She agreed. They fit together perfectly. He filled her, made her feel complete.

He drew back and thrust again, drawing a whimper from her.

Maddy wrapped her legs around his waist while he set a steady rhythm.

Parker nestled his face into the crook of her neck. He thrust harder, faster, while she clawed at his back.

His deep grunts and moans in her ear fueled her desire for him. She raised her legs higher, trying to meet him thrust for thrust.

She threw her head back in complete ecstasy.

Parker was pushing her to the edge again. She closed her eyes, unable to believe she could climax back-to-back.

"Maddy, I need you to come with me," he groaned. His hand slid between them. His fingers parted her folds and found her clit. He pumped harder into her while his finger strummed her little bundle of nerves.

Her breath caught in her throat when he brought her to completion again. Her muscles grew tight, and she crested.

Parker slammed his mouth onto hers as they reached their climax together. A warmth flooded her while he poured himself inside her.

Seconds turned into minutes, and the minutes seemed to morph into hours. She wasn't quite sure how much time really passed, but being with Parker erased all sense of time.

He rolled to the side, withdrawing his semi-soft

shaft from her. She protested, but he brought her flush against him and tucked her into his side.

They lay together without saying a word.

Everything was just too perfect. Two months ago, she wouldn't have believed she would ever have a civil conversation with Parker.

Now, she was in the circle of his arms, feeling safe and whole.

Tears formed in her eyes and slowly fell.

Parkers eyes opened, and he glanced down at her.

"Did I hurt you?" he asked. He tipped her chin up to force her to look at him. Concern lined his face while he waited for an answer.

"No, silly." She chuckled. She reached up and wiped her face.

"Then what is it? Tell me," he whispered.

She stared at him and shook her head. "I'm just feeling emotional. It all seems too perfect. Almost as if it's a dream," she admitted.

"Believe me, this is no dream. I'm real." He paused and brought her hand up, placing it over his chest. She could feel the steady beat of his heart underneath her hand. "Can you feel my heartbeat?"

She nodded, unable to form words.

"This between us is as real, Maddy. Just as I live and breathe, I promise you this is real."

"You don't think it's too fast?" she asked.

"Think of it like riding a horse," he murmured.

She rolled her eyes. Parker was too much like their son. Everything resorted back to horses.

"I'm serious. Our past was us falling off the horse. You know what we need to do to have our future?"

"What?"

"We have to get back in the saddle."

❧ 16 ❧

The sun's rays forced Parker to wake. A yawn overtook him. He attempted to stretch, but something heavy had his arm trapped. His eyes flew open, and he found Maddy still asleep where he'd tucked her in.

A smile spread at the memory of the night they had shared together. His Maddy hadn't believed him when he said he'd just need a quick nap. She was too tempting in that soft little nightie she had put on. Just watching her sleep, and feeling her curves pressed against him was enough to drive him crazy.

There was no way he was going to waste a night in bed with her and just sleep. Once in the park had not been enough. He'd awoken from his nap with a raging hard-on for Maddy. It gave a new meaning to the term morning wood. It had been too easy to slide down the bed, pull her little gown out of the way, and spread her legs wide open for him.

Her body responded to him perfectly.

It hadn't taken long for him to wake her from her slumber. One taste of what was between her thighs had him dying for more.

He glanced down at her, finding her with a smile on her lips. He tugged the covers up higher since they were both still very naked. He wouldn't want to chance Tyler walking in the room and finding them in all their glory.

Parker leaned down and pressed a kiss to Maddy's forehead. The scarf on her head was skewed. Some of her dark strands stuck out from underneath it. He wasn't sure what the point of it was, but he was sure she'd fix it when she woke up. He smiled at the soft snores escaping her lips.

She was beautiful.

A noise at the door caught his attention. He glanced up and found Tyler standing inside the doorway with a curious expression on his face.

Parker cleared his throat. "What's up, bud?"

Tyler stood there for a second, not saying anything. Parker wasn't sure what to think, but then Tyler answered.

"I was going to ask Mom if I can have some cereal."

Maddy stretched her hands in the air. She fell back against the pillows and opened her eyes. She followed his gaze and looked over her shoulder.

"Good morning, baby." She smiled while she turned over in bed, careful to not let the blanket fall away from her. "What's up?"

"Morning, Momma. Can I have some cereal?" he asked. His gaze flickered to Parker before settling on his mother.

"How about I cook us some breakfast? Would you like that?" she asked.

Tyler's face lit up. He jerked his head in a nod. "Can we have pancakes?"

"You betcha," she said. "Go on downstairs. We'll be down in a minute."

"Okay." He flew through the door and closed it behind him.

"Oh boy." Maddy rested a hand on her forehead.

"What's wrong?" Parker propped himself up on his elbow.

"I'm not sure it was a good thing for Tyler to see us in bed together." Her eyes were filled with worry.

Parker pulled her to him. He pressed a chaste kiss to her lips. He leaned away from her and brushed the wayward strands of hair from her face.

"Well, Maddy girl, he's going to have to get used to seeing me around. I'm not going anywhere." He kissed her again. Her body softened against his. He took advantage of her lips parting to slide his tongue inside her mouth.

His cock hardened and brushed her thigh.

"Parker," she gasped. She laughed and cupped his cheek with her hand. "We have to go. Our child is waiting downstairs."

He tried to kiss her again, but she ducked away from him. Her laughter filled the air as she attempted to roll away from him.

"Where do you think you're going?" he growled playfully. He tugged her back across the bed to him, trapping her beneath him. "That's much better."

"Parker, Tyler is going to be wondering what is taking us so long." She chuckled.

He reached up and snatched her scarf off her head. "I don't think this is doing its job anymore."

"Hey!" She cried out, falling into a fit of laughter. "You're going to mess my hair up."

"Me?" he scoffed. He leaned down and nuzzled her neck with this face. "You, my dear, were doing a perfect job of that on your own with as wild as you sleep."

He nibbled on her neck, and she screeched. She struggled to buck him off of her, but he pressed his weight down on her. He outweighed her, and was much stronger. He slid his hands along her side and paused.

"Don't you dare," she warned with her eyes growing wide.

Parker grinned. He'd forgotten she was extremely ticklish.

"What are you willing to do to get free?" he drawled. He drew one finger down her soft skin.

She jerked away from him.

She yelped and strained to push him away. "Please, don't make me scream." She giggled.

"Oh, now you don't want me to make you scream?" He chuckled. She'd challenged him earlier by saying she wasn't going to scream.

Parker Brooks never backed down from a challenge.

"Okay, okay!" she practically shouted. Tears fell out of her eyes as she tried to keep from laughing. "What do you want?"

Parker removed his hand from her side and trailed it down to her thigh. He pushed them to the side and rubbed the head of his cock against her slick opening.

"Let me in, baby." He brushed his lips over hers. Their son could wait. Right now, it was Parker who needed her the most.

She let loose a whimper. Her eyes fluttered closed. Her legs opened wider while she arched into him. He guided his cock along her slit, teasing her.

"Please, Maddy girl. Can I?" He slipped the tip inside and paused.

"God, yes!" She dug her nails into his ass and pulled him to her.

His cock sank deep, completely into her. A tremor snuck through his body at the sensation of her slick walls wrapping around him. He held his hips as still as possible while staring into her eyes. He slowly sat back on his heels and pressed her legs wide. He glanced down at where they were joined and gradually slid back inside her.

His gaze flickered to hers once he was settled.

"No. Screaming."

———

PARKER MADE HIS WAY DOWN THE STAIRS BEHIND Maddy. She looked over her shoulder at him with a smile on her lips. He chuckled at how skittish she appeared. She went into the living room with him close behind her.

She'd better run. He couldn't keep his hands off of her.

Their quiet sex had led to one of the most intense orgasms of his life. With much practice, he was sure they could nail down the no screaming clause while having a child in the house.

"Hey, buddy. You doing okay?" Maddy asked, walking over to Tyler. She removed his hat and pressed a kiss to his forehead.

"Yeah," he replied without taking his eyes off the television. "I'm starving, Mom."

"I know, I'm going now. Pancakes coming up!"

She spun around and met his gaze. He stood between her and the path to the kitchen.

"I'm hungry, too, Maddy." He winked at her.

She flushed and rolled her eyes. She brushed past

him and poked him in the side. "You should be good," she muttered.

He barked out a laugh, watching her disappear into the kitchen. He moved to the couch and sat next to Tyler. The television was on an old but good episode of *Bugs Bunny*.

It took Parker back to his childhood when he and his brothers had tried to watch Saturday morning cartoons. They'd wake up and eat breakfast, then try to get some television in, but their father made them go out to do chores on the ranch. They'd whine and groan, hating to go out to work, but Jonah Brooks' word was the law.

If it was time to do chores, then it was time to work.

"Can I come to the ranch?" Tyler asked as the show went to commercial. Tyler turned his attention to Parker.

"Sure. You're welcome to the ranch anytime," Parker said. His son wouldn't have to ask permission to come to The Blazing Eagle. It was as much his as it was Parker's. "We have plenty of horses for you to ride. We could go hunting, fishing, whatever you would want to do."

"How big is it?" Tyler asked. "Do y'all have ranch hands? Do you do cattle drives like on that show *Cattle Life*?"

Parker laughed. He raised his hand to stop the steady flow of questions.

"We own one of the largest ranches in the county.

We have a few ranch hands who work there all year round, and then we hire part-timers when we need more people. When you come out there, I'll have to introduce you around." He felt good being able to have an open conversation with his son. He hoped they would have a bond that would become tight. Tyler was a good kid, and he couldn't wait to introduce him to everyone. "As for that show, I've heard of it, but I've never watched it. I'm not sure if our version is the same as what they show."

"Momma lets me watch it. A cattle drive looks like hard work."

"That, it is." Parker nodded. "It can be dangerous. The cattle can be unpredictable. Everyone who participates in moving the cattle have to work as a team."

The show came back on, gaining Tyler's attention. Parker watched Tyler fiddle with his hat. He hadn't tried to put it back on when Maddy had taken it off. Parker figured out that Tyler had something on his mind. Parker would be patient and wait to see if Tyler would say whatever he was thinking.

The scent of bacon permeated the air. Parker's stomach growled. Maddy was banging around in the kitchen. She was singing a song off tune, and Parker chuckled.

Just being in their small home had him relaxed and as happy as he'd ever been.

It gave him a sense of home and family.

Parker sat back and imagined what it would be like if they moved into his home on the ranch. He pictured a little girl with dark pigtails running around after Tyler.

Parker's heart lurched with the vision.

"Can I ask you something?" Tyler asked, breaking the silence. He glanced over at Parker.

"Sure, buddy. You can always ask me anything," Parker encouraged. He rested his arm on the back of the couch and shifted toward Tyler.

"Are you and Mom dating now?"

Parker paused. He wasn't quite sure what they were calling what was between them. But Tyler was asking, so Parker was going to speak to his son, man-to-man. It wasn't easy for a kid to walk into his mother's room and find a man in her bed. Tyler had every right to ask what Parker's intentions were.

Parker could respect that.

"Well, to be honest, me and your mom are getting to know each other again. We are going to take it one day at a time and figure this out," he admitted. Parker offered a small smile to Tyler. "I want to get to know you, too. I would love for us to grow close and do father-son things with each other."

"I would like that, too," Tyler whispered. He looked down at his hands. A bashful expression came over his face. "Can I be honest about something?"

"Of course, bud. What's on your mind?"

"I don't know what to call you."

Parker froze in place. It was a tough pill to swallow hearing his son didn't know what to call him. They'd only just met, and would have to spend time with each other to form a father-son bond.

"Whatever you're comfortable with, bud. You can call me Parker, if you like." Parker's voice grew gruff. He was going to have to earn not only his son's trust, but the right to be called Dad.

It had been a week since Jonah had been rushed to the hospital. Parker and his brothers had been rotating coverage at the hospital. Their father had yet to wake up. The doctors were unsure as to why Jonah had not gained consciousness yet.

Even with the threat of the unknown with Jonah hanging over their heads, Parker was on cloud nine. He'd gotten to spend as much time with Tyler as he wanted. Maddy even let Tyler stay with him while she was working. He didn't like the fact that she had to work nights at The Tipsy Cow, but there was nothing he could do about it at the moment. She was even taking online classes. Parker didn't know how she had juggled being a single mother, work, and school.

It gave him a new respect for her. Maddy King was one tough woman.

He was proud of her.

Tyler was a natural on horses. He looked like someone who had been riding since he was born. They had some mares that were gentle enough for kids. They were the ones that worked with the kids in the camp.

But Parker wanted to find Tyler his own horse.

A man couldn't be a cowboy without his sidekick.

That was something Parker absolutely believed in, and he was going to get his boy one. He'd placed a few calls and was waiting to hear back.

It was going to be a surprise for Tyler.

He couldn't wait to see Tyler's face when he saw the steed.

Parker made his way out of the barn, and just like clockwork, Maddy and Tyler had arrived.

Parker took his gloves off and shoved them into his back pocket.

Tyler was sporting his new buckle. He ran full force toward Parker and barreled right into him. A slight groan escaped Parker, but the pain was worth it.

Tyler resembled a true cowboy now.

"Hey, buddy. How are you?" Parker asked. He returned the hug before Tyler stepped back.

"Can I ride now?" Tyler eyed some of the hands milling around out in the corrals. Excitement lined the boy's face. He never knew what he wanted to do when he got to the ranch. There was too much to pick from for an eager nine-year-old.

"Tyler King," Maddy scolded.

Parker winced hearing the last name.

"Where are your manners? He asked you a question."

A sheepish expression came over Tyler's face.

"I'm doing okay, Parker." Tyler smiled. "I'm really excited. I want to try riding Nightstar."

Parker chuckled. Nightstar was a great horse, young and playful. He was amazing with the kids, and was one of the star horses Wade used for camp.

"I'm sure we can arrange that." Parker glanced at Maddy. It had taken much coaxing to get her to step foot on Blazing Eagle land. He completely understood her reasoning behind it, but he wasn't going to have her not come to the ranch. He made a promise to her that things were going to change, and he meant it. "How are you, Maddy?"

She returned his smile and walked up to him. He tugged her close and pressed a kiss to her lips. He just couldn't enough of her. Her lips were delectable, but a certain nine-year-old was standing by them, so Parker had to keep the kisses short and sweet.

"Are you free today?" he asked. He entwined their hands and pulled her along with him.

"Yeah, I'm off today. Tyler has been driving me crazy since we got up, wanting to come here." She tucked her thick hair behind one ear as they walked.

"Come on, Tyler," Parker called out. "We can go

watch Rashad working on some training with one of the new horses we got."

"Cool." Tyler tagged along, following them.

They made it behind the barn where Rashad, one of the hands, was working with a new mare. They hadn't come up with an official name yet for her.

Tyler ran over to the fence and hopped up on it, becoming totally engrossed in Rashad and the horse.

Parker tried not to look at the spot where his father had collapsed, but his eyes automatically went there. They stood next to Tyler in silence.

"So, if you're off today, why don't we get you up on a horse, too?" Parker asked.

"What?" Maddy turned to him with wide eyes.

"Don't tell me you're still afraid." Parker chuckled.

"Mom, are you scared of horses?" Tyler asked.

"No." Maddy shook her head.

"Has your mother told you the story about the time she fell off a horse?" Parker asked Tyler.

Tyler's eyes grew round. He shook his head. "No. She never told me she'd ridden a horse before."

"Because it was a long time ago." Maddy grimaced.

"What happened?" Tyler's gaze flickered between Maddy and Parker.

Parker readjusted his hat and leaned against the fence. "Your mother and I had just gone fishing—"

"Mom, fishing?" Tyler gasped. He looked at Maddy as if she'd grown a second head.

"Yes, your mom has been fishing before. I grew up in a small town, so of course I know how to fish." Maddy folded her arms in front of her chest.

"Anyway, we rode horses to the creek. When it was time to come back, your mother was on her horse, and I was on mine. During the ride, your mother was trying to take pictures. Well, the horse apparently didn't like what your momma was doing, and before I knew it, your mother was on the ground."

Tyler fell into a fit of giggles. Maddy covered her face with her hands.

"How was I supposed to know the horse was going to keep moving?" she muttered.

"You didn't give her the command to stay." Parker shrugged. He turned to Tyler, who was hanging on to his every word. "And that was probably the last time your mother rode a horse. She wouldn't even get back on, and walked all the way back to the ranch."

"Mom!" Tyler groaned. He rolled his eyes and shook his head. "Everyone knows if you get thrown from a horse, you have to get back in the saddle."

"Y'all can laugh now, but I was traumatized." Maddy pouted.

Parker pulled her to him. He laid a kiss on the top of her head. "You were not."

"Can you teach me how to lasso? Uncle Wade said I had to practice a lot. I want to be really good so I can help teach other kids when camp starts." Tyler jumped down from the fence.

Wade was currently at the hospital, while Carson was working with a few other hands on the new gating system they'd ordered. Jonah had wanted to get the system to help contain the cattle, and it had arrived yesterday. The company had come and set them up. Carson had wanted to try it out with a few of the cattle.

"Sure, buddy. I have some—"

He was cut off the by the shrill ring of his cell phone. He pulled it out of his pocket, and Wade's name flashed across the screen.

"Yeah?" Parker answered.

"It's me. Come on up to the hospital. Dad is awake." Wade disconnected the call.

Parker released a curse. He glanced at Maddy and Tyler, who had openly listened to his side of the call. He dialed Carson, who answered on the first ring.

"Did Wade call you?" he asked without greeting.

"I just got the call," Carson replied, his voice grim. "I'm on my way back to the house. Go ahead without me. I'll be right behind you."

"I'm leaving now," Parker said. He hung up and turned back to Maddy and Tyler. "I got to get to the hospital. My father is awake."

There was a deep hesitation in him. He wasn't sure what was going to happen once he got to the hospital. He'd enjoyed this last week with his child. What would he say to the man who'd almost caused him to miss out on knowing about his son?

Maddy and Tyler glanced at each other. They shared a look before turning back to him.

"We're going with you," Maddy announced.

"Are you sure?" He couldn't ask them to stay at the hospital. He didn't know how long they would be there. "How about you head over to my house and hang out?"

"Parker, it's okay. We want to go with you." Maddy reached out and rested a hand on his arm.

"I may be there for a while—"

"We're family. We're going, too," Tyler interjected.

Parker paused and glanced at his son. His heart skipped a beat at Tyler's words.

We're family.

"You said that family always has each other's back. I'm going, too." Tyler folded his arms in front of his chest.

Maddy's eyes widened at Tyler.

Parker was proud of his boy.

"That's right." Parker cleared his throat. "Us Brooks men stick together."

Parker glanced at Maddy for the final decision.

She nodded to Tyler. "You heard him. Family sticks together."

"Well, then, let's go."

THEY MADE IT IN RECORD TIME TO THE HOSPITAL. The highway was clear, and there wasn't a deputy in sight, allowing Parker to drive a little faster than the speed limit.

Parker didn't know how, but Carson arrived a few minutes after they did.

He must have been driving like a bat out of Hell, Parker thought to himself.

They walked through the hospital and made it up to the same waiting area they had been in while Jonah was in surgery.

Wade was pacing the room when they entered. He paused at the sound of the door opening and turned to face them.

"It's about time," he muttered. His gaze flickered to Maddy and Tyler. His eyes softened. "Hey, Maddy. Hey, Tyler."

"Hey, Uncle Wade," Tyler said. He flew over to Wade and slammed into him.

Wade wrapped his arms around Tyler for a brief hug. "Thanks for coming, buddy."

"We dropped everything and came right away," Parker murmured. He enclosed his brother in a tight, manly hug, slapping him on the back.

Carson grabbed Wade in a bear hug afterward.

There was a slight tension hanging in the air on the ranch. Once word had gotten out about Jonah's condition, the hands were getting restless, waiting to find out about their boss.

"What's going on?" Carson asked.

"Come over here, Tyler. Let's take a seat." Maddy guided Tyler over to a row of chairs.

"He's awake right now. They are going to try to take that breathing tube out of his throat. Once they make sure he's stable, they said we could go back and visit him."

Parker nodded and glanced at Maddy and Tyler. He walked over and took a seat between the two of them. He needed them close, and he was glad they had come with him.

Anxiety filled him. He didn't know if he could go to the room and talk with Jonah. There was too much pain and unfinished business. His father was wrong for what he had done, but dammit, he didn't want him to die.

He wasn't sure they could mend the relationship, but at least he knew he wasn't the cause of Jonah's death.

The man had always been strong and mean as an ornery bull.

There had to be a reason why Jonah Brooks had survived.

Hell wasn't ready for him.

Time seemed to pass by slowly. The wait was killing Parker.

Finally, the door opened, and in walked Dr. Mizen and a few other staff.

"Hello, family," Dr. Mizen greeted.

Parker, Wade, and Carson stood and shook the doctor's hand.

"How's he doing, Doc?" Carson asked.

"So far, he's doing well off the vent. We wanted to make sure he wouldn't need it again. He's not out of the woods yet. Recovery is going to be hard. This was tough and beat him down, but I have a feeling your father is a fighter."

Parker snorted. The doctor didn't know Jonah Brooks.

"That, he is," Wade commented.

"We're going to keep him for another night here in ICU. If he's improved even more by morning, then we'll move him to the regular nursing floor."

"Thank, Doc." Carson held out his hand.

They each shook the doctor's hand and murmured their thanks.

"If you want to come see him now, we can allow two people at a time. Judy here can walk you back to him." Dr. Mizen motioned to the nurse at his side. He waved goodbye, and he and the other physicians stepped out of the room, except for Judy.

Parker nodded to Carson and Wade. "Y'all go ahead."

"Just follow me." Judy smiled.

Wade and Carson left the room with the nurse.

Parker took his seat again.

"Are you going to go see him?" Maddy asked.

Parker shook his head. He couldn't bring himself to stand in front of Jonah Brooks. This past week he'd been able to spend with Tyler and Maddy made him realize how much he would have missed.

"I can't ever forgive him for what he did," he muttered. He removed his hat and ran his hand through his thick curls.

"What he did was wrong." Maddy rubbed his leg with her hand. "But we're together now."

"I missed out on so much," Parker snapped. He pushed up from the chair and stood.

He'd missed out on the birth of his child.

He'd missed the first steps, the first tooth appearing, and potty training.

He should have been there to help raise his boy, to teach him things that he would need to know as he grew into a man.

He turned to Maddy and Tyler, who were both staring at him.

An idea hit him. Maybe he was crazy, but he knew what must be done.

The door opened to the waiting area. Wade appeared. He hadn't been gone long, but he returned looking more haggard and tired than before he'd left.

"Where's Carson?" Parker asked, not seeing his other brother behind Wade.

"He went to go get coffee." Wade blew out a deep breath.

"How is he?" Parker asked.

Wade shrugged and took a seat. "He's asking for you," he announced. He jerked his head toward Tyler. "And the boy."

Maddy stood abruptly. "I don't think that is a good idea. We were just here to support Parker. Tyler isn't ready to meet him yet."

Parker hesitated. He didn't want to subject Tyler to his father either. There was no telling where the old man's head was at after being in a coma for a week.

A small hand slid into his. Parker glanced down and found Tyler standing next to him.

"It's okay, Dad. We'll go in together."

Parker froze in place. His knees threatened to buckle.

The short time he'd spent with Tyler had meant the world to him. Getting to know his son was the most important thing to him. Parker peeked at Maddy, who had tears in her eyes. She nodded.

He peered back at Tyler. "Let's go, bud."

※ 18 ※

"Anytime you want to leave, you just say the word," Parker said.

He and Tyler stood outside the door to his father's room. Parker was starting to hate hospitals. He hoped it would be a long time before he'd have to ever come back to one.

"It's okay. We're together." Tyler stood taller.

"If you get scared, let me know. We'll leave immediately." Parker thought back to how his father had looked before with all the tubes running in and out of him. It could be a little intimidating for a child to see. The sight had plagued his dreams, and he wouldn't want Tyler to be affected by it.

"Did something bad happen between you and your dad?" Tyler asked, obviously picking up on Parker's hesitation to enter the room.

Parker eyed the busy nursing unit and let out a sigh.

"One day when you're older, I'll explain it to you." He reached out and rested a hand on Tyler's shoulder. Maddy had asked him about that day, and he hadn't shared it with her. The pain he'd felt was too raw to open again.

In the future, he and Maddy would have to come together and tell Tyler the truth of why Parker hadn't been around. They owed that to the kid. He was smart and intelligent, and Parker was lucky Tyler didn't hate him.

There was one thing for certain that Parker knew, though. He would never be the type of father Jonah was. He would always want what was best for his children, but Parker realized he could only teach them what was right and wrong. It would be up to them to wade through the shit life threw at them and make the best decision.

Parker removed his hat and held it in his hands. He took notice of Tyler doing the same. Parker held out his hand, and Tyler slid his smaller one into it.

They entered the private ICU room, with Parker leading the way. Jonah was propped up against the pillows with his eyes closed. The machines around him beeped softly. There weren't as many tubes going into his father as the last time he'd been there.

Parker stopped at the foot of the bed, with Tyler coming to stand next to him.

Jonah's eyes popped open. He stared at Parker for a moment. In the bed, Jonah appeared smaller than usual. He had always been a tall, stocky man, with the same hair color as Parker, only his was sprinkled with gray. Now he appeared as if he had gone twelve rounds with a prized fighter, and he was not the victor. Jonah's eyes, same as all the Brooks brothers', focused on Tyler.

He stared at Tyler for a moment, not saying a word.

Tyler returned the gaze with the curiosity of a child.

The room grew tense.

Jonah finally shifted his head away and glanced out the windows.

Parker shared a look with Tyler. His smaller hand squeezed Parker's for a brief moment.

In that second, Parker knew his little man was brave and would be fine. But Parker didn't relax. He was ready to protect his boy from any backlashing Jonah may try to give.

"He looks just like you when you were his age," Jonah said, breaking the silence. His voice was rough and strained. He turned back to face them. "Those eyes. He's definitely a Brooks."

Parker bit back a smartass retort, but he didn't want to argue in front of Tyler. He dare not tell his father Tyler didn't have their last name.

Not yet, at least. But it was for Maddy and Parker to work out. It was none of Jonah's business. He'd meddled enough in their lives. Parker was sure his father would have an issue with that, and Parker would have to put him in his place.

Hell, that was why they were in the hospital.

"What's your name, boy?" Jonah asked, shifting slightly as he settled back again.

"Tyler," his son responded, unintimidated.

Parker could have sworn Tyler stood taller. His boy had a stubborn streak, just like him. His little chin lifted.

"What's yours?"

Jonah's eyebrows rose. Parker watched his father closely, but all he saw was respect blooming in his eyes.

That was something hard to earn from Jonah.

Tyler was apparently every bit of Jonah as he was Parker.

"My name is Jonah. I'm your father's pa," he replied gruffly.

A deep cough rattled Jonah. His body shook as he tried to clear whatever was choking him. The monitor above the bed displayed his increasing heart rate.

"Water?" Parker asked. Slight panic rushed through him. After observing his father go down at the ranch, he couldn't witness something like that again. It messed a man up watching someone he cared about almost die. He moved to get the cup of water sitting on the bedside table, but Jonah held up his hand. He reached for the cup himself and took a sip.

Stubborn ass.

Jonah pulled himself together. His gaze flickered between the two of them. He cleared his throat and pushed himself up higher.

"There was a reason I wanted to bring you both here together," Jonah began. He took another sip of water. "I've done some things in my life I'm proud of, and that was raising three boys. I wasn't perfect by any means, but I did the best I knew how. All I ever wanted in life was to help my boys grow up into good men, pass down my legacy, and watch the fruits of my labor flourish."

"Pop," Parker sighed, but Jonah help up his hand, silencing him.

"There are some bad things I've done, the worst being my intervening in between you and Maddy, son. If Momma was here, she'd string me up. There's nothing I can say or do to reverse the past, but I wanted to speak to you two as a man and say I'm sorry." He shifted his gaze to Tyler. "I'm sorry your father wasn't around. If you ever want to blame anyone, put it on me."

Parker was stunned. He couldn't believe his father was sitting there in his hospital bed apologizing.

Hell had officially frozen over.

Jonah Brooks never apologized.

Ever.

"I'm sure Maddy doesn't want to speak with me, and I'm okay with it, seeing how I treated her. But whenever she is ready, I do want to speak with her," Jonah said.

"I'll let her know," Parker replied. That was all he could muster, because he was still in disbelief. The man in the bed resembled his father and sounded like him.

Almost dying must've made Jonah take a long hard look at his life.

But he knew Maddy would refuse. He was barely able to get her to the ranch. The damage Jonah did in a conversation ten years ago forever changed their lives. It would take a long time before any of them could truly get past what Jonah had done.

"I'm your grandpappy, Tyler, and I hope one day you can forgive me for what I've done."

Tyler stood still and nodded. He clutched his hat to his chest.

Parker had to keep his mouth from falling to the floor. He didn't know what had happened to his father while he'd been in that coma, but if he had to guess, he'd say that while he was teetering on the fence of death, he had a good scolding from Momma. There was no one around on the planet who could get through that thick skull of Jonah Brooks other than her.

"Pop, when you recover and you are doing better, we all need to sit down and hash some things out. I can't ever promise Maddy will be there, but we'll be there." Parker rested his hand on Tyler's shoulder, who nodded his agreement.

"I'd like that," Jonah said.

Parker glanced at the ceiling and smiled. *Thanks, Momma.*

He had a funny feeling that even though she wasn't here amongst them, she was watching over them.

―――――

MADDY STROLLED ALONG BEHIND PARKER AND TYLER toward the truck. It didn't go unnoticed that Tyler held on to his father's hand. It touched her heart that Tyler had called Parker *Dad*.

There hadn't been any rush for him to call Parker anything.

It had been her son's decision.

He was growing up so fast right before her eyes. If only time could slow just a little so she could enjoy these moments some more.

He'd acclimated so well with Parker coming into his life. He was always a happy boy, but now, he just beamed whenever Parker was around.

When they'd returned from visiting Jonah, something had changed between the two of them. They weren't gone long, but it would seem the pair had grown even closer. Tyler hadn't strayed far from his dad. They hadn't really mentioned anything while they'd lounged in the waiting area.

She wasn't sure what all was said in that room, but her curiosity was piqued.

"Come on, Mom," Tyler called out over his shoulder. "Why are you so far back?"

"Because I have short legs and can't keep up with you two." She laughed and increased her pace. She arrived at Tyler's side and took his other hand in hers. "So, what do y'all want for dinner?" she asked.

They had stayed at the hospital for a while. Jonah had been moved out of the intensive care unit.

It was getting close to dinnertime. They'd grabbed snacks from the cafeteria earlier, but it was nothing to hold her over. Her stomach was making itself known at the moment.

"Pizza!" Tyler chimed in.

"Pizza?" she echoed.

"I could go for a good slice myself. Why don't we go into town to the Pizzeria?" Tyler suggested. They arrived at the side of his truck. "My treat."

"Please, Mom? Can we? We haven't had pizza in a while." Tyler pushed his hat back away from his face, showing off his infamous sweet, begging expression.

"We just had pizza two weeks ago." She chuckled. Apparently, two weeks was considered a while to a child. She rolled her eyes. "Fine."

Parker opened the back door and helped Tyler into the truck. He shut the door and turned to her. He leaned against the passenger door and ran a hand along his face.

"What happened in the room?" she asked, no longer able to hold off asking.

"He took one look at Tyler and apologized. Man-to-man, he spoke with Tyler and told him outright that if there was anyone to blame for my absence, it was him." Parker sighed.

Maddy studied him, and took in all the emotions that fluttered across his face.

"Well, that was mighty big of him," she said slowly. She would have loved to have been a fly on the wall to hear that apology.

"You should have seen Tyler. He was brave, and handled himself well with my father." Parker smiled.

Maddy blew out a deep breath. She was so proud of her son. She wished she'd had half of his confidence. As a young woman, she hadn't been able to stand up to Jonah.

"Well, he is his father's son."

Parker's gaze flickered to hers. He jerked her to him and wrapped his arms around her. She returned his hug, basking in the feel of him.

"Maddy girl, I've been thinking." His deep voice rumbled underneath her ear.

"What is it?" She drew back slightly so she could tilt her head up to see him.

"I don't want to be apart from you and Tyler. I want you two to move in with me on the ranch."

"Parker, I don't know. We've only recently recon-nected." She chewed on her bottom lip.

Parker reached up and trailed a finger along her face. "Yes, that's true, but we've missed out on so much."

Maddy blinked back the tears that were forming. Her emotions were running rampant. She was in love with Parker, but did he love her? After a few months of parenting, would he want to give up? This was all new for him. What happened when he'd have to discipline Tyler? Or they got into a fight?

What then?

"Parker, that is a big decision you are asking me to make," she breathed.

"Tyler would love living on the ranch. You wouldn't have to work, and could focus on school full-time." He grabbed her face in his large hands and leaned down. He pressed a soft kiss to her lips. "We can be a family. I've missed out on so much, Maddy girl. Please?"

She melted against Parker. He knew all the right buttons to push with her. How could she resist? Every day, Tyler talked about this father nonstop. All the things they'd done on the ranch, the chores he was assigned to do, riding horses, and hanging with his uncles.

In that quick time, Tyler had fallen for The Blazing Eagle Ranch.

But, of course, it was in his blood.

She glanced at the window of the truck and found Tyler with his face pressed against the glass.

"Please, Mom!" he shouted. "Can we? Pretty please. I promise to always eat my vegetables!"

She turned back to Parker and found the same puppy dog face Tyler gave her when he wanted something.

"Give us a chance, Maddy girl."

She closed her eyes, and the walls and barriers in her broke.

"All right!" She laughed. "We'll move in with you!"

Parker released a shout just as Tyler did. He scooped down and picked her up and spun her around. He set her down and claimed her lips in a soft kiss.

"Maddy girl. You've given me everything I've ever wanted."

Her stomach chose that moment to release a growl. They both chuckled at the sound.

"Good. So take me and your child out and feed us," she demanded playfully.

"With pleasure."

"No peeking," Parker stressed.

Today was a big day. He'd had a few surprises up his sleeve. Maddy and Tyler had moved in with him two months ago. It felt good to have them under his roof. Tyler had taken to ranching like he'd been doing it his entire life. School was going to be starting soon, and he'd talked nonstop about making new friends and inviting them out to the ranch.

Maddy had cut back at The Tipsy Cow and only worked part-time. She insisted she was an independent woman, and still wanted to work while she took her classes. He'd tried to argue she didn't need the job, but his woman was damn stubborn.

What could he do but support her decision?

His father was in a skilled facility, and being as ornery as ever. He was going to be released next week, having completed rehab. The prolonged hospital stay had caused him to get deconditioned.

At the center, Parker was sure the nursing staff were going to have a party the minute Jonah was discharged. Parker and his brothers had made all the arrangements to have a home nurse visit to make sure he would be monitored.

As stubborn as Jonah was, Parker was sure his father would be trying to get back on his horse soon. According to the physicians, he was going to need to take it slow.

"But what if I trip?" Tyler asked.

Parker had blindfolded him, not wanting to give away the surprise.

"We're here. We won't let you fall." Maddy laughed. She walked alongside Tyler as they led him into the barn.

Carson and Wade stood in front of the stall where Tyler's gift was waiting, with shit-eating grins on their faces.

"Come on, buddy. Just a few more steps," Carson called out.

Parker guided Tyler in front of him where he could look into the stall.

"What is it?" Tyler bounced in place.

"Be patient. You're going to love it." Wade chuckled.

"Okay," Parker murmured. He glanced around the barn and grinned.

Maddy nodded at him. It was time to remove the blindfold.

Parker untied the bandana and took it off.

"Surprise!" they all shouted.

Tyler's gaze locked on his gift. His mouth dropped open, and he turned to Parker and Maddy with a huge grin.

"That's mine?" he shrieked. "Really?"

There in the stall was a fourteen-hand gelding. Parker had found him as a rescue. The horse was twenty-one years old, and had worked cattle his entire life. He was experienced, and would be a great first horse for Tyler to own.

"This is unbelievable!" Tyler yelled, jumping in place. He flew around and wrapped his arms around Parker in a tight hug.

Parker barked out a laugh at Tyler's excitement. It had taken him awhile to find the perfect horse for his son. He wanted one that could be teached, and be patient with Tyler as well. The ranch where Parker purchased the animal had practically given him away.

He wrapped his arms around Tyler and returned the fierce hug.

"I hope you like him. He'll be a real good fit for you for your first horse," Parker said.

"Thank you, Dad. This is the best gift ever." He threw himself at Maddy next.

She released a grunt and hugged and kissed on him.

"Thank you, Mom."

"You are quite welcome. Now, I hope you know your dad and I will be expecting you to take care of him," Maddy said. "This is a big responsibility."

"I will." He leaned against the door of the stall, staring at the horse. "What's his name?"

"His name is Rocky," Parker replied. He couldn't wipe away his grin if he tried. He remembered the day he'd received his first horse. He'd practically had the same reaction. They all had. It was almost tradition in the Brooks family to be gifted a horse as a child.

"That's a mighty fine horse." Wade slapped Tyler on the shoulder. "You'll have to show him off to the children in the camp."

Tyler loved the camp, and spending time with Wade and the kids who participated. He'd made a lot of friends. He was considered the popular kid in the group since he got to live on the ranch. There was so much for them to do. They all moaned and groaned when it was time to go home.

"Now you'll have your own horse to go out and repair fences and check on cattle with us," Carson added.

"This is so cool." Tyler shook his head in disbelief.

"Well, we have another surprise for you," Parker announced. He peeked at Maddy before focusing back on Tyler.

His son turned around in shock.

"There's more?" he gasped. The poor kid didn't look like he could handle any more, but what they had next for him was important.

Maddy stepped over to Parker. He wrapped an arm around her. She slipped a piece of paper from her pocket and handed it to Tyler. Parker squeezed her shoulder and pressed a kiss to the top of her head.

Tyler opened it and froze in place. He scanned the paper, and immediately, tears ran down his face.

Parker felt a little tickle at the back of his throat.

"What does it say?" Carson asked softly.

Tyler sniffed. He glanced up at Parker with his lips trembling.

"It says that my name is now Tyler Brooks." His voice ended in a sob. He rushed forward, allowing Maddy and Parker to envelop him in their arms.

Carson and Wade whooped and hollered.

Parker cleared his throat. He knew what his boy was going through. He'd almost had the same reaction when he and Maddy talked about it. She'd immediately agreed. When they got the official paper, Parker had stared at it for hours. Just seeing his last name attached to his son brought out feelings he couldn't even begin to describe.

"Why the tears?" Parker asked.

Tyler stepped back and rubbed his face on the sleeve of his shirt. "I'm just so happy. Now I can really say I'm a Brooks cowboy." He smiled.

"You were always a Brooks, and now it's official." Maddy wiped the wetness from his cheeks with her hand.

"Speaking of official..." Parker cleared his throat.

His brothers snickered behind him. They were the only two who knew of this next secret. He tugged Maddy to him and held on to her hand.

"What's going on?" she asked suspiciously. She looked from him to his brothers, narrowing her gaze on them. "What are y'all up to?"

Parker reached into his front pocket and took out the little black velvet box he'd had hidden.

"Maddy girl," he began. He fought through the stiffness and got down on one knee in front of her. He was going to do this properly, and the pain in his knee was not going to stop him.

Maddy's eyes filled with tears. She was the most beautiful woman he'd ever known. She was an amazing mother to their child, and he didn't want to spend his life with anyone else but her.

"Parker," she whispered.

He tightened his grip on her hand as he opened the box, displaying the custom-made, flawless, three-carat diamond engagement ring.

"Will you marry me?" He didn't need any long, drawn-out poem or romantic words. Maddy knew how he felt about her. He ensured that not a day went by that she didn't know.

"Yes!" she cried.

He stood and wrapped his arms around her.

He was the happiest man around. He had the woman he loved and a son he adored. He couldn't ask for anything else.

Wade, Carson, and Tyler cheered and clapped.

In front of his brothers and his son, there was no better place for him to ask the woman he loved to marry him.

He took the ring out of the box and slid it onto her finger.

"I love you, Maddy girl," Parker murmured, staring into her beautiful brown eyes.

"I love you, too, Parker."

He bent down and kissed her.

Wade, Carson, and Tyler all came around, hugging and congratulating them.

"It's about time." Wade chuckled.

"Welcome to the family, Maddy." Carson leaned over and pressed a kiss to Maddy's cheek.

Parker kept an arm around her, not wanting to let her go. The guys were speaking with Tyler about the supplies he would need for his new horse, and running him out to get the proper sized saddle for him.

Maddy gazed down at the ring on her hand that rested on his chest and sighed. "Since we are making everything official, I just want to let you know that we'll have to get married soon so this baby will be born offi-cially as a Brooks."

Parker froze in place.

"Maddy girl, are you saying what I think you're saying?" His hands shook as they slid down to her soft round belly.

"You, Mr. Brooks, are about to be a daddy again." Her lips spread into a wide grin. She covered his hand with hers.

He reached down and picked her up, swinging her around as he shouted his joy.

Today was a day of many surprises.

———

Loved Parker and Maddy's story? Then go ahead and download Wade's story! He's up next in Roping a Cowboy. Click HERE now!

PEYTON'S FREEBIE

Sign up for my mailing list and get your free copy of Tempest: His Best Friend's Sister Romance! This book is not published anywhere! It's my gift to you!

Click here to get started: PEYTON'S GIFT

She was his best friend's sister and should have been off-limits.

Rashad Mays was a ranch hand on the Blazing Eagle Ranch. He had grown up in Shady Springs and had no intention of leaving. This was his home, and he was ready to settle down. Only the woman that captured his eye was the sister of his best friend, Nate.

There were unspoken rules between friends when it came to their little sisters--don't touch.

Yani Polk was not like other women. She didn't chase after cowboys for a casual roll in the hay. She was a lady. Sexy, curvy, successful, and currently the star of his late-night fantasies.

He'd thought he would be able to push her out of his mind, but when she came strolling onto the ranch, he couldn't resist. Her smile and the gentle sway of her hips called to him.

The sizzling attraction was too great to resist. Rashad did the unthinkable. He broke the rules.

Yani was the woman for him, and he was willing to fight to prove it.

———

Want to meet Rashad?
Download Knockin' the Boots today!

A NOTE FROM THE AUTHOR

Dear reader,

Thank you for taking the time to read Back in the Saddle. This is a first in series and I am so excited to bring you the men of Blazing Eagle Ranch. I'm planning for at least three books, but this will depend on readers response. This means I need to hear from you!

If you loved Parker and Maddy and want to continue on getting more books in this world, leave a review! If you don't know what to say, just say, "Peyton keep this series going!"

Warm wishes,

Peyton Banks

ABOUT THE AUTHOR

USA TODAY Bestselling author, Peyton Banks, is the alter ego of a city girl who is a romantic at heart. Her mornings consist of coffee and daydreaming up the next steamy romance book ideas. She loves spinning romantic tales of hot alpha males and the women they love. Make sure you check her out!

Sign up for Peyton's Newsletter to find out the latest releases, giveaways and news! Click HERE to sign up!

Want to know the latest about Peyton Banks? Follow her online:

Cowboy, Take Me Away

Hard to Forget

<u>Special Weapons & Tactics Series</u>

Dirty Tactics (Special Weapons & Tactics 1)

Dirty Ballistics (Special Weapons & Tactics 2)

Dirty Operations (Special Weapons & Tactics 3)

Dirty Alliance (Special Weapons & Tactics 4)

Dirty Justice (Special Weapons & Tactics 5)

Dirty Trust (Special Weapons & Tactics 6)

Dirty Secrets (Special Weapons & Tactics 7)

Dirty Ultimatum (Special Weapons & Tactics 8)

<u>SWAT boxset, books 1-3</u>

<u>Trust & Honor Series (BWWM)</u>

Dallas

Dalton

<u>A Langdale Christmas</u>

The Christmas Secret

The Christmas Wish

The Christmas Gift

<u>Interracial Romances (BWWM)</u>

Pieces of Me

Hard Love

Retain Me

Silent Deception

<u>African American Romance</u>

Breaking The Rules

<u>Mafia Romance</u>

Unexpected Allies (The Tokhan Bratva 1)